Addiction
Wild Crows
Book 1

Blandine P. Martin

Author's Note – Please Read

Wild Crows is a story born from shadows and strength. It explores dark and gritty realities, and while every scene has its place in the emotional journey of the characters, some content may be triggering to sensitive readers.

If you're in a vulnerable place, I encourage you to take care of yourself and read this story only if you feel safe doing so.

Content Warnings:

This book includes:

– Gun violence

– Physical assault

– Drug use and trafficking

– Sexual assault (one explicit scene of rape)

– Death and grief

– Strong language

– Criminal activity

Reader discretion is advised.

proofreadinfg: Sherri S.

Book cover by Blandine P. Martin, photo (shutterstock)

https://blandinepmartin.com

For dreamers,
Because there's nothing impossible if you believe in
yourself, if your work hard and if you have faith in life and
its beauty.

1

JOE

I still remember the day when I borrowed one of the most beautiful dresses from her closet. I was nine or ten. Perched on stilettos far too big for me, I decided to entertain my mother with a fashion show, just like the ones I had seen on TV. I had selected two outfits. Unable to choose between the one with the black straps and the other made of red velvet, I opted for both. That was me. I was always second-guessing myself.

I can still remember the crystal-clear laugh that came from our living room. It belonged to my biggest fan. Just remembering that moment made me smile. With her long, wavy blonde hair and her round cheeks, she looked like a goddess. She also sounded like one with her voice's smooth notes.

My grandmother once told her to stop calling me Joe — it was too boyish for a little girl, she said. My mom just smiled, defiant. Joe was perfect. Josephine for close friends, and Joe for everyday life. Besides, I was more of a daredevil than most little boys. My mom and I shared the same adventurous, slightly offbeat spirit.

She was my model, my mainstay, and a perfect copy of myself. Fierce as a lioness, she had overcome many obstacles, starting with being a single mother. Only a few men had won her heart, but those cowards had all left her. The last one, a guy named Dwayne, had escaped in the wee hours of the morning without an explanation, despite an idyllic relationship that had lasted for several months.

It destroyed her. And why had this man left? Unfortunately, I knew why. The reason was the same that had brought me there that morning. All the happy memories were replaced by an irrepressible feeling of injustice. Why her? For more than sixty years, my mom's health had been irreproachable, and still, fate had decided to give her one last rough ride. That damned blight had eaten her away, starting with her lungs.

Despite her disease, she never let herself go. She always kept the same smile that will forever be engraved in my memory. She was exhausted due to the endless treatments, but she kept on saying that everything would be alright. I believed her. Maybe more for my sake than hers. It had been a long road, full of doubts and false hope, especially when she finally went into remission. But there were always recurrences to bring us back to reality. My mom had passed away, and I had to deal with the administrative hassle caused by her death.

"Mrs. Blake?"

From the other side of the desk, a woman wearing a

grey suit was watching me. With a quizzical look, she politely instructed me to stop daydreaming. I wish I could have run away far from here. She gave me an accommodating smile, and I gazed around the room as if I didn't know where I was. Parts of the walls were made of polished wood, and next to the window, at the far end of the room, antique bookcases were filled with years of archived files.

"Thanks for coming," she continued.

I nodded, not entirely sure I was actually there. The executor opened a file on which the name "Margaret Blake" was written. At that moment, reality hit me. I couldn't escape it. I noticed that the dark blond bob sported by the woman in front of me was perfectly coordinated with her thick and very classical glasses.

She took a deep breath, and then she spoke. "We are here to open and read the will written by your mom."

I felt uneasy when she referred to the woman who had raised me as *Mom*. I felt like the word was inappropriate to define her. In my opinion, I was the only person who could use it. It had a whole different meaning when I said it. It carried the love I felt for her and that nagging pain that would follow me forever. Nevertheless, I didn't say anything. I nodded politely to end this unpleasant meeting as soon as possible.

"In her will, Mrs. Blake stated that she leaves you her house."

It wasn't a surprise. My mother had prepared me for this. She had always kept me informed, even though it was unbearable for me to talk about her death at that time. I acknowledged the news silently. Mrs. Dorsay turned some documents towards me and handed me a pen.

"If you agree with the terms, you need to sign at the bottom of each page."

A throbbing pain, rising from somewhere deep inside my stomach, reached my throat. Putting that damned scribble on these few sheets of paper meant so much more to me. It meant that I accepted her death, and I suddenly realized I would never see her again. My stomach was in knots, and I wiped a tear with the back of my sleeve. Then I leaned towards the file in front of me. I remained focused, taking my time while I reviewed all the details mentioned in the document. Never had a signature been so traumatic. Even though the executor was probably used to these human tragedies, she noticed my distress and showed empathy when she seized the signed sheets. She gave me the keys, and I carefully put them into my bag—as if they represented something private or special that needed to be protected from the outside.

"Fine," the executor said efficiently. "You will receive a copy within a week. Your mother also left a personal letter for you."

Uneasily, I looked at the envelope she was holding in her hands. Once again, I scribbled my signature on a piece of paper to acknowledge that I had received it in person and on that specific day. We sorted out the last details of the will, but a part of me had already left for a faraway place, lost in sweet memories of when my mother was still alive.

Unable to feel any emotion, I turned on the engine of my old black Comet. Its distinctive and familiar roaring sound soothed my broken heart. I was looking for a refuge in my little cocoon, trying to forget about the rest of the world. The sealed envelope was lying on the passenger seat over a pile of documents. I wasn't ready to open it yet. I couldn't summon the strength to read the farewell note my mother had taken the time to write. Without a word, I glanced away and sped off as fast as I could.

2

JOE

Absentmindedly, I walked through the door. I had grown up there and came back two years ago so I could give my mom her daily medication. I had to give up having my own place. It didn't matter. I had broken up with Arthur, my boyfriend, and I needed a change. My mother and I completed each other. Together, we were stronger. I gave her all my love, and I tried to share all the positive energy I had in my heart. She had that special healing effect on me. All my sorrows disappeared when she was by my side.

She was like that magic kiss one gives a child to make a booboo disappear in a heartbeat. Now, this huge house seemed so lonely, like lost in time. My mother had made sure that everything was taken care of before embarking on her last journey. Nothing had been left unattended, even when she was living her final moments. I knew why she had done it before she passed away. She was worried about me, and she wanted to protect me, her only child. She had time to plan the aftermath of her illness during those long months when she was not feeling well. Every administrative and logistical detail had been taken care of. One last time, she protected me as the loving and devoted mother she had always been.

I swallowed hard. In the living room, I headed for the big blue sofa, and I collapsed on it, completely exhausted. I threw the pile of documents, including the envelope that the executor had given me, on the pillow next to me. Why had she bothered writing a letter to me? Was it another farewell? We had already talked about everything and even more. Why would she do that, especially when she always told me we would see each other again? I swallowed hard. Suddenly, my curiosity became too strong to resist, even stronger than the overwhelming fear and pain that was torturing me. This envelope was sending me a silent message, like a merciless mermaid song that I couldn't ignore any longer. I grumbled.

I looked around the room. There was always that dead silence that reminded me, every damned second, my mom wasn't coming back. It was like an old tune played by a lousy fateful hand, a reality that I was still not ready to accept. My head was throbbing, and the unpleasant sensation finally consumed every part of my body. I could feel its presence in every part of the house, and it was upsetting.

I knew every stage of the grieving process perfectly. It was basic knowledge for a person working in a hospital's psychology department. Undoubtedly, I was going through the denial stage. It was the first one of the stages, just after what was termed "aftershock." Soon, rage would follow. I could almost feel it. At that moment, I felt like I was drowning, and the light coming from the surface was gradually disappearing. All parents must die someday, but nothing could have prepared me for this tragedy. I doubted that one could get over it.

In the house, time seemed to be frozen. I could almost hear the ghosts of my childhood and their happy laughter, like a memory of the past. Hesitantly, I turned my attention to the envelope.

I gave in.

"What couldn't you tell me?"

I was talking to myself like a mad woman, so I laughed bitterly. Then, I had a meltdown. Holding my breath, I grabbed this thing that was tormenting me, and I tore it open. With the utmost care, I unfolded the piece of paper filled with feminine and elegant handwriting. Just imagining its content gave me the chills. As I was reading the first words, tears flooded down my cheeks. Through each word I read, I could hear the voice of my mom speaking to me.

My sweet little Joe,

I know you well enough to imagine the pain you are going through while you are reading these words. Yet, I can assure you that everything is alright.

The time has come for me to go to heaven. You, my sweetheart, need to move on and hold your head up high to face what life has in store for you.

Your heart is so big. It needs to be filled with love. And this is the reason why I feel it's time for me to confess. The void left by my departure needs to be filled by someone else. Loneliness is not for you. You are full of love, and it is crucial that you share it with someone. You can't stay alone for the rest of your life.

Here I am, twenty-seven years after life granted me the most beautiful gift I could hope for. You. You never dared to ask the most critical question of all, probably because you thought it would hurt my feelings. Or maybe because you were afraid to be disappointed. Now, the time has come. If you decide to ignore this, I'll respect your choice. Still, I am convinced it will help you heal. If you trust me, please read on, Joe, my sweet girl.

Your father's name is Jerry Welsh.

I paused to wipe down the flow of tears that prevented me from seeing clearly, and I tried to regulate my erratic breathing. I had to rest for a few moments to deal with all these words that had never been said.

The last I heard of him, he had a small shop in Monty Valley, California. He is not aware of your existence, sweetheart, and I will forever bear the burden of this secret. I don't feel sorry for myself or even for him, but for you. It was too late when I realized that I had made the wrong choice and that his absence would create a void in my life. I'm the only person who should be held responsible. I acted as a mother who needed to protect her child. But I failed.

Today, I hope there is still time to patch things up and to make up for the biggest mistake of my life. I know it's a bit late, but I've never found the strength to stir up the past.

I know you have this strength, Joe. You have the courage I lack. You must admit that you are a hothead. You got it from him.

Go and find your father, sweetheart. If you must, give him this letter. He might be surprised at first. He will probably be shocked or even get angry. Then he might feel overwhelmed, but it doesn't matter. The truth can no longer be denied. You have his eyes, Joe, his determination, and his temper, too. Time will help you heal. I am sure of it. Please, trust me one last time, sweetheart. The future is yours.

It's almost time to go. Take care of yourself, and don't push away those who will try to help you. The healthy young woman you have become is the biggest pride of my life. I love you to the moon and back. Someday, we will meet again in heaven. Until then, live your life to its fullest. Enjoy every second of it, and show everyone what you are made of. Keep on moving on and fight for everything you believe in. It will help you achieve your dreams.

I love you.
Mom.

For a moment, I held my breath, torn between shock and sadness. These last few words made me feel like my mom was abandoning me one more time. A wave of unidentifiable emotions overcame me. My eyes filled with tears, for these words were too difficult to accept. Some of them were still echoing in my sore head. Two of them, especially. A name and a surname: Jerry Welsh. My father.

Completely lost, I flinched. I was a shadow of myself. The shadow of a little girl facing the tough choices she would have to make soon.

3

JOE

My eyes looked through the smoke of the black liquid I was holding in my hands to keep them warm. The Short Break Lounge was crowded. Most of the staff met at this cozy lounge during their breaks, mainly because it was very close to the Stonebridge Hospital. My break was almost over. That morning, I'd had trouble staying focused, but I had a good reason. With my heart still in pieces, I had come back to work at the beginning of the week.

Besides the pain caused by my mother's death, my thoughts were consumed entirely but the contents of the letter. Maybe it was a trick played by my subconscious to keep me from overthinking. Could a single piece of paper change my life forever? I vaguely heard the high-pitched voice of my colleague, Saddie, but I wasn't paying attention. Usually, her weird intonations made me smile. She was the closest friend I had then. I really liked her, and the feeling was mutual. Still, I had not been myself since the day I had read the words written by my mother. A part of me was buried in endless questions, fear, and hope, and it seemed like this feeling was not about to go away.

When her cold fingers touched mine, I jumped.

"Are you listening to me? Yes... no?"

Saddie looked daggers at me.

"Hum... Of course I am... Why would you say that?" I said in a confident tone.

My friend sighed.

"Listen! I know what you are going through. You really should take a step back and ask yourself the right questions."

"I know. I won't make any hasty decision."

She looked at me doubtfully.

"Are you sure? The last few days, you've been kind of absent... like you are already gone."

I took a deep breath, realizing she was right. I vaguely tried to explain my feelings. "I'm simply trying to make sense of all this... I can't stop asking myself what would happen if I woke up thirty years from now without having met him."

My father. I had been obsessing over him for the past week. I guess I needed to finally know. I knew I had to see him. In my colleague's bright blue eyes, I detected a glimmer of embarrassment. She was nervously rubbing her hands against each other.

"What will you do if...he doesn't want to speak to you?" Saddie asked.

She immediately apologized. She probably realized

that she was crushing all my hopes. I wasn't stupid. Being twenty-seven years old, I had learned to protect myself from the dangers of life. If things turned out that way, I would recover. I would be hurt, but I would survive.

"I guess he has his own life," I said. "And a family, too. It will certainly shake him."

"Yeah... twenty-seven years without hearing a word... It's crazy!"

I nodded silently. My mouth was craving the hot, steaming coffee in front of me.

"If he doesn't want to get to know me, I will accept it... I guess. There is nothing else I can do."

With a pout on her doll-like face, Saddie watched me silently. "Whatever you decide, don't throw everything away without being sure. It's too risky. Many people do that, and they regret it afterward. You'd better ask Sullivan if you could be granted an *unpaid* leave." She made air quotes as she glanced at the colored sign displaying the lounge's name.

I laughed for the first time in many days. But Saddie was Saddie. She had this gift to lift my spirits up when I felt down.

"Then, if it doesn't go as planned, you'll be able to come back to your old life, and you'll have your job at the hospital."

"I still haven't decided yet, I..."

"Come on, you know you have to!" she said defiantly.

Then she looked at me accusingly, and I laughed again.

"I think you have a great life," Saddie continued. "You have a good job, an amazing friend, a great apartment, and then we can eat the best tacos in town. Oh, I forgot to mention, a horrible ex-boyfriend, even though he is super sexy, and he is still in the game ...Arthur, still in the game?"

"No." My voice was sharper than usual.

I broke up with Arthur Marvel two years ago. But I still couldn't talk about him without being angry and disgusted. I couldn't forgive his lies and deceptions. After living together for a year and a half, I had left, even though I was not entirely over him. Sometime after this, my mom's disease and my job changed my priorities. I put my love life aside. Of course, I had a few relationships, but nothing serious. I didn't have the time nor the will to be involved with someone else anyway, and clearly, I lacked the ability to trust again.

Not after everything that had happened. For the last few months of our relationship, my dear Arthur had been sending me sweet messages. But I knew those clumsy attempts to win me back only occurred when he was out partying at a late hour. The not-so-perfect structural engineer was spending more time living in luxury than working on building sites. As for me, I had decided to stay away from him. No man could fool me twice. I tried to follow this golden rule to protect myself. But being an optimist, Saddie liked to remind me that a relationship with Arthur was still possible and that the man might have changed. But I didn't agree.

"I'll give you the good job, the amazing colleague, and the Mexican food," I concluded.

To stop the conversation on that painful chapter of my life, I dipped my lips into the hot coffee.

"How long will you be away?" Saddie asked.

"I don't know. It depends... on this man, Jerry..."

"I guess. Anyway, it's gonna be weird not to spend my breaks with you."

"What I can tell you is I'm not going to miss the roller-coaster floor! I was thinking about asking for a transfer, anyway."

Visibly surprised, Saddie nodded without judging me. "And what does this Jerry do for a living?"

"He's a hotel manager, according to my mom..."

"California..."

As she pronounced the word, I could see she was traveling there in her mind.

"So, you are leaving Oregon for California. Is it about a day's drive?"

"Yep!" I confirmed with an amused smile on my face.

"Really? That's all? ... When I think California, I picture the sun at the end of the journey..."

"Exactly."

"Still, Monty Valley sounds like a shithole," she continued.

"There are no shitholes around San Francisco," I corrected, laughing.

I saw Saddie's shoulders drop. Then she raised her cup, and we cheered as if we were already saying goodbye.

"What about your mom's house?" she asked.

I hadn't thought about it. Or, to put it succinctly, I hadn't quite decided what the next step was.

"I don't know. I don't feel like selling it right now. Too many memories... But living in it is a whole different ball game." I winced before I continued sharing my thoughts with her. "At least, not yet... This trip to California might put me on the right path. When I come back, I will have had enough time to make the right choice."

Saddie was looking at me with a sweet and encouraging expression on her face. I smiled with melancholy. I was grateful to her.

"I am keeping my fingers crossed, honey," she said.

We drank our coffees and shared an enormous donut covered with pink glazing and colorful sugary dots. Then it was time for the sexy redhead to go back to work. We hugged each other. Even if I kept saying I would make my final decision in a few days, I knew deep inside that I would give in. The word "Daddy" was calling me relentlessly. The pain caused by thirty years of ignoring his identity was overwhelming, and I needed to put a face on this name. Yet, I had learned how to live without a father.

Over the years, all the questions that kept coming to my mind when I was a child had been fading away. But at that moment, they were coming back because of my mom's words in her posthumous letter. These words were bringing down all the walls I had built to protect myself. It was time to face life on my own. I had an opportunity to meet the man who was responsible for my presence on earth.

I slammed the door of the Short Break and decided to walk Saddie to the hospital. I had to see my boss and have a little chat with her.

4

JOE

My suitcase felt like a dead weight. In my defense, I didn't know what I would need to take with me. California weather would be milder, but apart from that, I didn't have the slightest idea of how many clothes I should bring with me, as I was unsure how things would turn out. In my luggage, I had placed an old family album filled with pictures of myself and my mom since I was born and the letter she had left me. When I double-locked the door, I shot a last glance at the house in which I had taken my first steps. I wouldn't be gone forever, but just the idea of leaving it behind, even for a short period, made me nostalgic.

I took a deep breath, and I convinced myself it was time to go. I was nervous. A thousand scenarios were going through my head. I turned on the engine of my old black Mercury Comet. It was the only valuable thing I owned.

No pricey jewelry, no big bank account, but a classic car my mom had bought when she was a hippie. It had been an impulse purchase and a sentimental one. I loved its design, the sound of the engine, and its character. But above all, it was something from my mom that was still alive. Its roaring sound was distinctive and unique. I drove away, leaving behind my family's cocoon to meet the unknown.

I had almost seven hours of driving ahead of me. The first hours went by relatively quickly as I listened to Bob Dylan and the Stones with my windows down, feeling the wind of freedom blowing through my hair. But I was just pretending not to be nervous. I knew it perfectly. My doubts would come back towards the end of the journey. Therefore, I tried to enjoy my first hours on the road. It was going to be a beautiful day. The first rays of light were coming through the windshield, and they were warming up my hands on the steering wheel. Unconsciously, I was saying my farewells to the green hills and the big lakes of my home state. Well, goodbye would be more appropriate. I would be back. "When" was the only question?

I made a stop around noon. The first part of the journey had whetted my appetite. A roadside stop did the trick. I had a burger, a few fries, and a soda. It was a breach of my usual healthy lifestyle, but it was tasty. I left a tip to the young and friendly waitress and continued my long journey with a cup of coffee in my hand. That's what I needed to get me through the next three hours of driving.

The scenery was changing progressively. The green mountains turned into dark golden hills. It was still the same wild landscape untouched by the human hand, but this time, the hot and dry air indicated that I was heading south. As I was driving through the small town of Corning, I spotted a road sign that announced what was coming next: in less than fifty miles, I would have to embrace my destiny. The anxiety I'd been feeling since leaving Oregon was intensifying and consuming me completely. I had to try to keep my mind clear to slow down the rhythm of my pounding heart. Forty miles left. I still had to drive through a few cities before arriving at my destination. A little town called Orland, and its white oak, willows, and red brick buildings. Ten miles left. The research I had done before leaving Oregon told me exactly where I could find this Jerry Welsh.

I had entered all the details in my GPS. I was now following its instructions so I could meet this father I had never seen before. All this seemed unreal, but it was happening. I continued to listen to my GPS and turned right at the crossing. Five miles left. A road sign welcomed me to Monty Valley. For a second, I couldn't breathe. I had arrived in a typical small city, with its apartment complexes dating from the '70s and flower beds along the sidewalks. A little bit further, I saw a residential area made of patches of cookie-cutter houses. The sun was burning hot, and the warm breeze that was coming through my half-open window made me feel like I was arriving at a holiday resort. I was in the valley. At the next light, I turned left and drove along a small river.

"You've arrived at your destination," my GPS informed me.

I parked on the side of the road and turned off the engine. When I looked around, my mouth hung open. I could see a bar, a motel, and what seemed like an automotive workshop in the distance. I didn't know if any of this belonged to my father, but if it did, he had more than one string to his bow, even if the buildings looked dilapidated and dirty. The moment of truth had come, and my fear was overwhelming. For a second, I was a lost child, frightened by the world around her and this adult I was about to meet. All the questions I had on my mind tormented me more intensely.

His name was relentlessly spinning in my head. My hands trembling, I got out of my old Comet and walked on California land for the first time. I breathed in and out multiple times, thinking it would calm me down. Bullshit! I walked hesitantly towards the big parking lot behind the fence and entered through the wide-open electric entry gate. Then, I took the direction of the bar, thinking I would have more chances to find a human soul. Unfortunately, the door was locked. I looked inside, and I saw a varnished wooden countertop like those you see in Irish pubs. I knocked several times, but no one answered. Then, I tried my luck at the hotel. There was no reception desk. I guessed customers had to check in at the bar, but it was locked too....

Finally, I turned around and scanned the vast deserted parking lot. My watch indicated that it was almost 5 p.m. The bar would probably open soon. I hoped I was right. I didn't feel like waiting. Suddenly, I heard a metallic sound from the workshop at the far end of the parking lot. It was my last chance. Intimidated by the thought of facing a father who had no clue I existed, the walk toward the shed seemed endless despite its relative proximity. I wiped my sweaty hands on my jeans and pulled on my jacket to hide my nervousness. I discovered a workshop through two retracted metallic shutters.

"Hello ...," I shouted.

I heard the metallic sound once again. Then I saw two legs dressed in overalls. A pair of used cowboy boots were sticking out from under an old Chevrolet.

"Excuse me... Hello," I repeated.

Grumbling, the guy who was working under the car slid on his creeper wheel-board to emerge from his hiding spot. Then he got to his feet. He was built like a wrestler, and his hair was tied in a ponytail that reached his elbow. Grease and dirt hardened the features of his face. A few wrinkles made me guess he was in his forties. I spotted a faded tattoo under the undershirt he was wearing beneath his half-open overalls. I cleared my throat as he was looking me up and down.

"Hello," he said in a deep voice. "Can I help you?"

"Yes. I am looking for Jerry Welsh. I thought I would find him here," I said in a shaky voice.

I noticed I had caught his attention.

"Jerry Welsh? And you are..."

"A family member," I said evasively.

He peered at me, probably trying to figure out if I was telling the truth. Then, his eyes turned to a small glass-windowed office at the far corner of the workshop.

"He's not in yet. He should be here any minute. You can wait in his office if you want."

. . .

I hesitated for a second and finally decided it wouldn't be a smart choice. Being alone in the back of a dusty workshop with a shady, muscular giant was not a safe option. I politely declined and informed him I would be waiting outside. He shrugged and returned to his creeper wheel board to resume his work under the Chevrolet. I breathed out and felt that my stress level was getting lower. I leaned against the exterior steel wall, and I waited for the arrival of the man who would change my life forever. Maybe I should say the man who was about to see his life turned upside down. Five minutes went by, and I already couldn't stand any more of that deafening silence that was only disturbed by the metallic melody made by the mechanic's tools and a few singing crows perched in a nearby tree.

Suddenly, I heard a roaring sound growing louder and louder. Soon after, I saw a big black motorbike driving into a narrow path bordering the complex. The biker had a Harley Davidson between his legs and a basic helmet on his head. I noticed he was quickly caught up by two other men who looked exactly like him. The trio looked like the Hells Angels, and they only slowed down when they got close to the main gate. I couldn't decide if I found them fascinating or frightening. I didn't trust that kind of bad boy. They had a reputation. And there I was, by myself, like an idiot. I wished my father could have been there at that moment. It would have given me a good reason not to be standing there, waiting for god knows what, in front of the shed at sunset.

Feeling down on my luck, I saw the three bikers drive to the shed. They parked in a perfect line. Their eyes were hidden behind sunglasses, but I sensed they were staring at me. They almost simultaneously removed their helmets, and I shivered. The first guy had short gray curls that were almost white. He was probably the oldest of them all. The second one had messy black hair. He couldn't be much younger than his friend. The third man was bald, and he had a big tattoo on his neck. Who would get a tattoo there? They got off their bikes, and I felt a presence behind me. The mechanic was there, and he was greeting the three other guys with a manly embrace. I felt entirely out of place. I wished my father would show up. I had a bad feeling. I was scared.

The oldest man walked to me. Despite his gangster look, he had a friendly smile on his bearded face. The other two guys followed him, acting like the tough guys they seemed to be.

"Hello, Can I help you?" the older man asked.

The mechanic spoke before I could utter a word. "The young lady here pretends to be a relative of yours..."

I couldn't believe it...

So, this guy, who looked like a fugitive, was Jerry Welsh. He was my father. I wasn't prepared for this. Things weren't playing out in my favor. The man in his fifties squinted, then he cocked his head.

"You didn't tell us you had such good genes," the bald guy said, laughing from behind Jerry.

He didn't react, and I started to regret my decision. Dropping such a bombshell on this man, surrounded by three fearsome bodyguards, might not have been such a good idea after all. I wished I could find a quick solution, and I decided to push my luck.

"It's a long story," I said without looking directly at him."Can we talk? Privately."

A wicked smile appeared on the square jaw of the tall, black-haired man standing on my left. But there was no trace of irony on the face of the man I was talking to. With his hand, he indicated the direction of his office. This time, I accepted his offer, relieved to leave the other guys behind. Not that I trusted this man, but confessing wasn't going to erase my fear of his intentions.

The worst that could happen would be to be kicked out of there. At least I would still have my dignity, and I would be able to go back to my car without listening to his friends' offensive comments.

"This way, babe."

The disgusting nickname made me shiver. Then, I walked through the glass door that had intimidated me fifteen minutes before.

5

JOE

Jerry Welsh closed the door behind him. I discovered a small room furnished with a metal desk covered with loosely stacked sheets and an old and dusty computer. There was also a broken armchair and a chair reserved for visitors. On the yellow-plastered walls, a few posters featuring naked playmates were displayed. There was no doubt I had landed in a low-class repair shop. He pointed out the chair to me while he sprawled on the rolling chair behind the desk. Then, he crossed his hands and studied me like I was an alien from outer space. I noticed the big silver rings on his large fingers, and I sat, not really knowing what to say.

"Stop bullshitting me. I've never seen you before, Sweetheart..." he said in a deep voice.

I was probably as pale as a ghost as I faced this heavily built man who looked like a highly trained veteran.

Despite his age, the muscles showing under his t-shirt and his leather jacket were impressive.

I could've gotten his number, called him, tried to find him when I got here... but after my mom died, all I wanted was to jump into the unknown. I needed an adventure—something she would've loved. I wanted to come face-to-face with him. I wanted to look him in the eyes when I told him I was his daughter, just to see how he'd react. Words can lie. A look can't

"I am not bullshitting you," I said. "To tell you the truth, I don't even know how to say this... But I swear I've given it some thought during my eight-hour drive."

Surprised, he raised an eyebrow. I wondered if he was thinking about my long journey. If so, there was more to come!

My eyes fixed on his puzzled face. I started to speak hesitantly. "My mother passed away last week..."

The creases on his forehead got deeper, and he raised his hand to stop me. "I am sorry, kiddo, but I can't help you. You're barking up the wrong tree if you are after money or anything else."

I took a deep breath to settle my nerves. "I don't want any money or anything from you," I corrected him. "My mother left me a letter in which she mentioned the name of my biological father." I hesitated for a second, and then I spilled the beans — just like that. Doing it differently would have been too easy. "And it seems you are that man."

It was straightforward. For a minute, the big gray-haired man in front of me watched me as if I were a lunatic who had just escaped from the asylum. I had to speak out right away, or else I would lose my chance to explain myself.

"Margaret Blake," I added. "Her name was Margaret Blake."

Jerry froze and then relaxed for a moment. My mother's name seemed to ring a bell. Suddenly, he turned pale.

"Mag... Maggie...?" he whispered.

I nodded and grabbed the opportunity to speak.

"Yes. I was born in 1990 in Stonebridge, Oregon."

He collapsed against the back of his rolling chair and looked at me pensively. Then, he passed his hand over his mouth. The blow hadn't been fatal, but the piece of news was apparently hard to swallow. I had brought up his past and thrown it to his face.

"You... You..."

He was not his arrogant old self anymore. He was just a helpless man, dealing with the information I had just given him.

"Yes, I know," I said. "It had been a shock for me too. I never thought I would meet you one day..."

Stunned, he didn't move a finger.

"I know my mother never told you about me. I can't imagine how you must feel ..."

He sighed. He passed his hand over his face and through his hair. The ruthless biker was no match for what I had dropped on him. I should have been proud of myself! But his embarrassment was hard to watch. I felt sorry for him... I felt like an old file everyone would rather leave untouched. But now, it was too late. I knew who my father was, or at least what he looked like. And he was nothing like what I had imagined.

Jerry Welsh cleared his throat several times. Either his eyes seemed lost, or they examined me attentively.

"I wasn't prepared for this..."

Still in shock, he paused for a moment.

"Did you come from Stonebridge just to see me?" he managed to articulate.

I nodded, and a smile came across his face. Then, he laid his eyes full of sadness on me. "I remember Maggie... But it was so long ago."

A brighter light was shining in his eyes. Had he been in love with my mother, or was it the news of her death that made him so sad? Maybe both.

I saw him straighten up in his seat. "No, I didn't know about you. I am sorry..."

"Me neither. I had never heard about you before. We are on the same boat."

My attempt at being funny brought a smile to his lips. Humor was my only defense against being overwhelmed by my emotions. In my teenage years, I frequently thought about my estranged father, but my mother always refused to answer my questions. She would tell me it was for my own good. And now, the man was standing in front of me, and he was as intimidated as I was.

"I have... a family," he explained in a gentler voice. "A wife and a son."

I cut him off. "A son... wow. So, I have a ... brother."

Still reflecting on his words, I suddenly realized what was bothering him.

"I didn't come here looking for trouble," I said. "After all these years, I just wanted to get to know you."

He looked surprised, or at least that's what I thought.

"I guess you want to stay in town for a while?"

I shrugged. I didn't want my father to see how eager I was to get to know him. I didn't want to scare him off.

"For a while, if you don't mind," I said.

Again, his hand stroked his face. He was probably thinking about how I was about to turn his life upside down. I couldn't tell him, but I was feeling exactly the same way.

"I am not going to ask you to go back to where you come from," he said. "After driving all day long."

It was my first victory. My father was tolerating my presence around him, at least momentarily.

"I'm just wondering how I am going to explain this to my wife... It's totally insane."

"I know... I feel the same," I reminded him.

"Where are you staying?" he asked.

"You mean in Oregon...?"

"No, here. Have you found a hotel?"

"To be honest, I came straight here. I am going to find something nearby."

He raised his hand to stop me from talking. "There's a small apartment above the bar. It's free. You can stay there."

It was more than I had hoped for. I was speechless.

"What's your name?" he asked.

"Joe. Well, Josephine," I explained with a smirk.

I hated my name. I had always preferred my nickname.

I saw a smile beneath my father's salt-and-pepper beard. "Coming from your mom, it doesn't surprise me. It was thirty years ago, but I still remember," he admitted in a sad voice. "She loved music, art, and the movies. A real hippie."

He was right. There was no doubt about it. The man standing in front of me had known my mom, even if it had been for a short period of time before I was born.

Suddenly, his expression became more serious. "How did she..."

"Die?" I mumbled. "Cancer."

"Fuck," he grumbled with his fist clenched on his desk.

"Yep. A damn lousy disease," I added.

"I'm sorry."

He stared at me for a moment before looking down. The big guy in front of me was trying to control his emotions. Decency dressed in a leather jacket.

"Thanks," I said.

Jerry Welsh got up and walked around his desk. Then, he bent over, right in front of me, stroking his mouth, and I could see a thousand questions in his eyes. He breathed in heavily.

"So, I have a daughter..."

"And I have a father..."

A quick smile formed on his lips, and I noticed a dimple on his poorly shaven cheek. "I need some time to get used to the idea."

"I understand."

"And to share the news with my family," he said.

"I get it."

I looked through the window and saw that other men had joined the ones I had seen before.

"So, you have a bar, a motel, and a workshop. And on top of that, you run a motorcycle club?"

Suddenly, I realized we were having a casual chat. I felt embarrassed, and my cheeks felt terribly hot. Jerry seemed to notice, and he smiled at me.

"Yep."

Then, he cocked his head and nodded. "I'm a busy man."

"Impressive."

"Would you like a tour?"

Touched, I accepted his offer. "With pleasure."

I wasn't sincere. I was eager to learn more about my father, but I didn't want to see his fellow bikers. And my guess was they were inseparable.

6

We left his office and met with the rest of the group. There were about ten men now gathered around us, looking at me with intense curiosity. I noticed that Jerry was glaring at two of them with menacing eyes. No one dared to speak up. I felt slightly embarrassed as I was standing right in front of them.

Then, Jerry spoke. "Is everyone here?" he asked.

A guy with long grey hair answered immediately. "Foxy and Hanger are not here yet. They should be in any minute now."

"As soon as they arrive, you brief them. I want them to be informed before they put their feet under the table."

Puzzled, some men were exchanging looks. Others were watching me, probably wondering why I was there. I felt out of place. I was surrounded by guys with leather jackets, cowboy boots, chains, scarves, tattoos, sunglasses, and big rings. With my jeans and my sneakers, I almost looked like a choir girl lost amongst a pack of wolves.

"Now, listen to me, guys!"

They all fell silent, waiting for Jerry to talk. "Something like this doesn't happen every day…" Then, he shook his head, probably searching for the words that would best describe a situation he hadn't acknowledged yet. "This young lady is my daughter," he said, pointing his finger at me.

One of the bikers, who was sipping a drink from a plastic bottle, spat out unexpectedly, which caused the guy standing in front of him to leap away. One of the bikers with dark curls left his bike and came a little bit closer to me. His eyes went from my legs to my breasts, and finally, he studied my face.

Stunned, he turned to Jerry. "Really? She's… your daughter? No kidding!"

He started laughing but stopped when he saw the menacing expression on his boss's face.

"Ash, get the fuck out of here!" Jerry said.

The tough guy swallowed hard and went back to his motorcycle.

"So… you're serious?"

The man talking was a forty-year-old guy with spiky blond hair.

"I'm dead serious, Mack. I've just had the information…"

"And you are sure you are the father?" said a guy with a beard on the right.

Jerry looked at me for a moment and gave a firm nod. "Absolutely."

"Damn..."

I suddenly realized I was the center of attention. What could be more unnerving than being a clueless young woman scrutinized by dozens of suspicious looks?

"My name is Joe," I added, probably looking like an idiot.

Jerry stepped forward, putting himself between me and them, and I disappeared into his shadow. He clenched his fist, and the atmosphere became electric. Some of the guys seemed to understand the threat.

"I'll make myself clear, guys. I will tear off the balls of the first one of you I see hitting on her or even looking at her in a way I don't like! You keep your hands in your pockets, and when I say your hands, I also mean your dicks. Roger that?"

He was such a poet! I coughed to remind my newfound father I was listening. I certainly looked like a poor, helpless thing in front of these heavily built men, but I didn't want to be over-protected either. That said, I thought it would be interesting to know more about their backgrounds, and I admired my father's authority and the respect he inspired. None of the guys protested. They nodded gravely, and their eyes looked in every direction except mine.

"Come on," Jerry concluded as he put his hand on my shoulder.

Speechless, I followed him outside the workshop. The night was about to fall, and for the first time, I felt somewhat safe around these men. A light breeze started to blow, and I wished I had brought a warmer jacket. California was warmer than Oregon, but fall evenings were chilly. We walked along the motel's rooms to reach the bar. I had time to examine more closely the embroidered patch on the back of Jerry's jacket. It was impressive. There was a stylish crow, a compass indicating the west, and two banners. Across the first one, one could read the name of the club, Wild Crows, while on the second banner, "Monty Valley 1975" was embroidered. I assumed it referred to the year the club was formed. He unlocked the door, and we walked into a room that smelled of alcohol. The neon lights blinked a few times before lighting up the bar.

Keeping it clean was apparently not their priority. I imagined there was no need to bother with details like hygiene or the bad smell left by the excesses of the previous nights. I heard footsteps behind me, indicating that the group of bikers had followed us. Jerry's warning kept them away from me, which suited me perfectly. He walked around the counter and served several beers. The guys closed in, and each of them sat down in front of a mug. I voluntarily stayed at the other end of the counter. Jerry handed me a drink, but I turned it down. When I leaned against the wooden surface, my hands got stuck. I jerked up and swiped my hands on my jeans. Jerry drank half of his glass straight down before slamming it on the counter.

"Sorry for the mess. One of the waitresses left without notice, and now I am screwed. Mona can't do it all by herself."

With a hand wave, I dismissed his apology. "No problem."

Then, his eyes froze, and he pinched himself while

looking at me. His men were talking to each other, ignoring me. They apparently followed their leader's instructions to the letter.

"You haven't told me what you do for a living," he said.

"I'm a nurse."

"In Stonebridge?"

"Yes. Well, I was working as a nurse. I negotiated unpaid leave with my boss. I didn't know how long I would stay..."

The crusty gray-haired man nodded. I guess it was his way of acknowledging my answer. I would probably have to get used to it.

"Have you ever worked as a waitress?"

His question surprised me.

"Yes. I waited tables to pay for college when I was younger."

"In that case, maybe you could give me a hand for a little while..."

Was I dreaming, or had my father just found a way to take advantage of me? Working as a waitress... after years of being employed in a hospital. The culture shock would be violent. Those were two completely different worlds. I couldn't say serving drinks to drunken bikers was my dream job! Yet, it would be the best way to get to know him and spend time in his company. Wasn't that the reason why I had crossed the state border? I pouted my lips and shrugged.

"Why not...?" I replied after a long pause. It was too late. The words were out of my mouth, and I couldn't take them back. "Temporarily," I added.

Jerry's bright smile illuminated his square face. He looked at his watch.

"Mona should be in any minute now. I'll need to tell her about you..."

"She's your... wife?"

I tried to keep a casual tone, but I suddenly felt shy. Generally, I needed some time to open up to people. I would probably need even more with my father...

"Yeah, she's my lady," he said in a funny voice.

I couldn't tell if he was serious. Jerry nodded and grumbled. "When can you start?"

"I don't really have anything planned," I reminded him.

He hesitated for a second. Then he let out a big breath before sharing his thoughts with me. "It should be crowded tonight. I need an extra. Give me an hour. Just the time to talk to my wife. If things go well, she'll brief you on what needs to be done tonight."

"It works for me."

He looked at me for a moment. "You must be exhausted after this long drive."

I shrugged. Of course, I was. But I didn't want to let my father know. I wanted to spend as much time with him as I could.

"I'll be fine," I reassured him, accompanying my words with a dismissive wave of my hand.

"Great. On Saturday nights, we never have a real meal. It's always a rush hour right after we open. If you're hungry, ask Pacho to fix you something. He's a good guy. He should be here any minute too."

"Is he the cook?"

Jerry nodded.

"Okay. Thanks for the info."

My stomach grumbled, and I realized the burger I had for lunch was long gone.

"Now, I am going to show you the apartment where you can stay while you're here. Well, if that's what you want."

I could stay. I was going to stay with my father. It was a brand-new and unsettling sensation, but it was real. I nodded and followed him as his crew looked at me suspiciously. I heard a bell sound as we were walking out of the bar, and I noticed for the first time the neon sign above the door. The Devil's Trip. It was the kind of name that made you think twice before walking in. It was intimidating, but this was the place where the last living member of my family was, and I wouldn't go away.

We climbed wooden stairs, and Jerry stopped on the third floor. There were several rooms for rent on the first two floors, whereas the apartment in front of which we were standing seemed to occupy the whole top floor. Jerry slid the key into the keyhole and he unlocked the door. He walked in first to turn on the lights in the narrow corridor, and I followed him. On the other end of an entry hall, there was a cozy living room furnished with an old sofa and a decent TV in front of a large armchair.

I thanked Jerry, who replied with a smirk. "I'll let you get comfortable. Come down when you are ready."

Then he left. What was happening to me was insane. Totally insane! I had just met my father, and an hour later, I was settling down to a new life. I had been so afraid of being rejected. I still couldn't believe it. Luck seemed to be on my side, which was highly unusual. Willing to discover my new dwelling, I walked around. The far end of the living room opened onto a small kitchen that had everything I needed. I was surprised to find coffee and a bit of food in a cupboard.

Overall, the place was clean compared to the bar downstairs. I walked on. At the end of the corridor, there was a small but functional bathroom. The walls were painted white, which matched the wooden cabinets. Behind the side door, I found my bedroom. The walls were painted beige, and it was furnished with a big, comfortable bed. A large window overlooked a shed. I opened the closet doors and found hangers waiting to be used. After my little inspection tour, I went back to the living room. Staring into the distance, I tried to get used to the idea that I would call this place home for quite a while. Then, I placed the keys on the kitchen counter and took a deep breath.

"Here I am, Mommy. I made it," I whispered to myself.

7

JOE

I took some time to get my stuff out of the trunk of my
Comet and bring it back to the apartment. It felt
strange to put my clothes into the closet. Moving in
was a big deal to me. Everything was so different from
what I had known so far and the life I still had the day
before. Saddie, my childhood home, and my mom seemed
so distant. Now, I was physically close to my father, who
would be my only family on this earth. I felt relieved that
he seemed to accept the situation. How could he deal with
it? It was unbelievable, and still... He must have been the
kind of man who went through a lot to get back on his feet,
just like that. The clock on the microwave indicated five
after six.

I had to keep moving. I was so tired my muscles were
aching, but I decided to ignore it. I would have time to rest
later. Right now, the most important thing was spending

time with my father. And if it meant giving him a hand at the bar, that's what I would do. I knew it was my only chance. After such a long drive to come and see him, I had to do everything I could to nurture this budding relationship. I did take the time to enjoy a nice shower and change clothes. After putting on a jacket and locking the door behind me, I ran down the wooden stairs. Jerry's daughter or not, I didn't trust these men. Not at all.

When I arrived, the Devil's Trip's red neon sign was still blinking, and it reminded me what type of place it was. I tried to comfort myself, thinking it was a trick of my imagination. I pushed the glass door, and I immediately felt the intense heat coming from within. The place was already crowded. Most of the tables were taken, mostly by men, but there were a few women here and there. Leather jackets and scarves from the nineties seemed to be must-have items around there. Folk-country music was being blasted through two huge loudspeakers. Feeling nervous, I walked through the room with a few pairs of eyes following me. I didn't bother looking back and headed straight to Jerry, who was leaning against the bar. When he spotted me, he shot a glance at the woman standing on the other side of the counter. I immediately understood it. Jerry gave me an awkward but friendly smile. He put his hand on my shoulder and turned to the lady I guessed was his wife.

"Joe, this is Mona," Jerry said.

"His woman," she added.

I gave her a reassuring smile before shaking her hand.

"Nice to meet you."

"Same here."

Mona's broad smile was both warm and defiant. I would have to prove myself to her. It made sense. Jerry swiftly walked around the counter and kissed her on the cheek before whispering in her ear. Feeling uncomfortable, I looked away.

"Come-on. Follow me," my new mother-in-law told me."I am going to show you around."

Jerry winked at me, and he walked back to return to the main room. Embarrassed, I joined Mona. I had entered her life without notice, and I was the living proof of her husband's past. A past she might have preferred to ignore, and that explained her reluctant smile. I guessed Mona was in her fifties. She had long black hair tied in a bumped-up ponytail, which made her look like a pin-up. Large, gleaming earrings framed a flawlessly made-up face, etched with the marks of time.

Her black rock-n-roll clothes made her look younger.

She was a beautiful woman in her own way. First, she showed me how the bottles were organized. I immediately reassured her by telling her I had already worked behind a bar and that I knew the basics. I told her I could use all the machines without reading the notice and that I was able to prepare all the basic mixed drinks. She seemed relieved not to have to teach me everything from scratch.

"You are going to be useful around here," she whispered to me while taking out a rack full of clean glasses from the machine. "Saturday nights can be crazy. They all come for the show. When I'm by myself behind the bar, it's difficult. We need a third waitress, but we haven't found anyone reliable yet.."

I nodded politely, but curiosity was eating me up. "What show?"

Mona paused. My question seemed to unsettle her. "What has Jerry told you exactly?"

I tried to figure out the meaning of her words. "What do you mean?"

Her amused laughter didn't reassure me. "What did he tell you about what's going on here?"

I took a deep breath, feeling a bit anxious about what she was about to tell me. "He told me he was the president of a motorcycle club and that he was in charge of the bar, the motel, and the workshop."

"That's right. But I am talking more specifically about the Devil's Trip."

"What about it?"

I felt as if all my doubts were about to be confirmed, and I didn't like it.

"Sweetheart, you are in a striptease bar. Well, at least on Saturday nights. It helps us fill the cash register."

Perfect! I couldn't believe my ears. My father was running a motorcycle club and a striptease bar. I was secretly hoping I wouldn't discover more shady stuff concerning this place. I tried to keep a detached attitude in front of the woman, who was now my mother-in-law, but she noticed I was troubled.

"So, they are all here for the show," I concluded.

"That's right!" she answered just before starting to laugh out loud.

Then, I met the famous Pacho. He was a strong and tanned man with round cheeks, probably in his forties. He offered me a snack that I accepted cheerfully. A few minutes later, he brought me the best enchiladas I had ever eaten, with a smile on his face. After I devoured them standing in front of the counter, I brought back the empty plate and called him "The god of enchiladas."

I decided he would be an ally around here. When I returned to the bar, I found Mona holding a notebook in her hand. She placed it in front of me and looked at me defiantly.

"Show me what you are made of, Miss Oregon."

Annoyed by the nickname she just had given me, I went on to do my job and showed her how professional I was.

From the corner of my eye, I saw Mona bring a fully loaded tray to a table at the far end of the room. I would certainly need a bit more practice to do the same. Then, two men dressed in leather jackets came to the counter. The first one was a tall, blond guy with a small beard. His head was shaven on the sides, and he had tattoos on his neck and on his forearms. I had seen him at the workshop earlier on. He was in his forties and walked too confidently with a charming smile on his face.

Next to him, I recognized the fifty-year-old man with black locks. A couple ordered two beers, and I served them at the other end of the bar. By the time I came back to the men, Mona was already there. The tall, dark-haired man hugged her and kissed her on the forehead. I was a bit surprised by their intimacy. Then, the blond guy kissed her on the cheek.

"So, you hired the new girl in town?" the blonde said, looking in my direction.

Mona turned to me with a broad smile on her face

before nodding to satisfy the men's curiosity. Annoyed to be considered an object, I took a step forward to be on the same level as Mona.

"That would be me. The new girl," I said with a fake smile. "Joe."

"I wasn't really asking, Joe. Jerry's daughter," the blond guy said jokingly.

With his arrogant gaze, I immediately pegged him as a ladies' man, the type who thrived on showing off. That was likely his strategy—seducing beautiful women he could parade around. I wasn't prejudiced, but he was an open book. I despised that kind of macho posturing and, more broadly, men who saw women as trophies.

"Joe, let me introduce you to Mack and Ash," said Mona.

I politely greeted them. The guys ordered drinks. Mona and I served them. Then, three girls joined them, bringing along pitchers full of beer. Once again, I felt out of place. I didn't have a leather jacket or tattoos. On top of that, I was wearing too many clothes to look like these women, who seemed to be groupies.

One of them was wearing Daisy Duke denim shorts that didn't fully cover her ass. Not only was she showing off her bare legs, she had knotted her unbuttoned blouse over her belly button so everyone could see her bra.

Her two girlfriends seemed to share the same taste for minimal clothing. But that's not what shocked me the most. One of them went directly to Mack, acting as if she was his girlfriend–which was plausible–while the other two embraced Ash, the older guy, in a very suggestive way.

I quickly glanced at Mona, but she had already left to take an order.

"Girls, this is Joe. Be nice! She's new around here. She's the boss' daughter," the ladies' man introduced me to his girlfriends.

I smiled politely to remain professional. I was here to work, and they were customers. It was the right thing to do, and I was new around there. I had to prove myself. It would be a bad idea to be hated by Jerry's men if I wanted to stay around him. The pretty but heavily made-up blond stuck on Mack's shoulders smiled at me and said hello.

The girls next to Ash just looked at me to see who everyone was talking about. Nice! One of them whispered something in the biker's ear, and he smiled. I was suffocating in this room, but I forced myself to stay calm. I had to keep my emotions under control. The gap between our worlds was widening, but if I wanted to get to know my father, I had to cross it.

Then, catcalls came from the crowd. The lights became dim, and the heavy curtains, blocking the view of the stage, opened mechanically. Two girls dressed up as schoolgirls with high heels appeared. All eyes were fixed on them. A folk song was playing, and I thought I recognized the suave voice. I was clueless about motorcycles and their shady business, but folk-country classics had been part of my playlist for years. When the girls on stage started to peel off their clothes, one could almost taste the testosterone in the air. Naked, the baby dolls came down towards the tables, and suggestive words began to fly around. I took a deep breath. Neither Mack nor Ash were paying attention to the show. They probably were used to it. Curious, I watched it.

Suddenly, Mona nudged me before leaning towards me. "You'll get used to it, Sweetheart. Our world is totally different from yours."

When she winked at me, I wondered: What was her story? How did she meet my father? Had he seduced her before she fell into his arms dressed in a leather jacket? Did it happen before the Wild Crows? She seemed to be at ease in this environment dominated by males.

I couldn't resist asking her a few questions. "Are these girls..."

"Hookers?" she said, cutting me off with a defiant look. "Yeah."

Mona seemed lost in her thoughts for a moment. "A hooker gets some money for her services, so the answer is no."

I almost choked.

"I am not sure I follow..."

My newfound mother-in-law rolled her eyes, probably thinking I was naïve. I didn't care. Getting information from this woman seemed a better idea than speaking to my cocky customers. With a mischievous smile on her lips, she explained.

"Let's say that if we take money out of the equation, yes, you can call them hookers."

I was a bit shocked by her harsh words and her amused tone, but I made sure I kept my emotions to myself.

"So, they sell their bodies without being paid?"

It didn't make sense, but Mona clarified it for me. "Sweetheart, these girls would kill each other to become the regular of one of the men sitting at the bar. Do you get it now?"

Wow!

I was speechless. And the word she used, "regular," made me think of a regular job and not of a serious relationship between two adults. These women were considered objects. Were they even aware of it? Obviously not. Did they know how ordinary people lived outside of the club and its strange rules?

"Why?" I dared to ask after a few seconds.

My father's wife shrugged as if everything she told me was natural. "They are the Wild Crows, Sweetheart. They are gods in this town. They take care of everything around here. They own the whole county."

I said nothing, but I realized I had stepped into an unknown universe with its own secret rules. It was vulgar to the point of disturbing. After a little while, I figured out Mona's place in that chaotic world.

"So, they want to be like... you?"

The way she always called me "sweetheart" encouraged me to speak more casually to her.

"I guess. Men call them 'sweeties.' They are a bit like candies that soothe them. It suits these women. They are ready to do anything to be chosen. I can tell you I earned my spot," Mona said with pride, looking into the distance. "Your father was a Don Juan. Girls were attracted to him like magnets. But I was the only one not to bow down. I suppose he doesn't like things that come easily to him."

"A good point for him," I concluded.

We smiled at each other in a friendly way. It was weird. Everything around there was. Not to mention that the whole day was strange. That morning, I had woken up wanting to meet my real father after twenty years of silence, and he had offered to shelter me in exchange for my help at the bar, which I had accepted as if it was the most natural thing to do. Next, I met Mona. Behind her tough attitude and her sharp tongue, she seemed to be a woman familiar to people, but more importantly, she had accepted me with open arms. I had to give my all to belong to my father's world. From now on, he would be part of my life. I was sure of that, and I wanted to be part of his.

After attending to a customer, Mona came back. "It's a totally different world, Joe. There are codes to respect. A hierarchy, too. I'll teach you if you want."

Puzzled, I looked at her. "Thanks."

"You're welcome. Now, go and take the order of the people who have just walked in. We don't pay you to chat all night long."

After winking at me one last time, Mona left and went to change the beer keg with the help of Mack, who had just dismissed his sweetie.

"You'll see," Ash said. "You'll get it, kiddo. Ain't that complicated."

Surprised to hear such a smooth and yet rasping voice, I turned around to face the biker. He must have been in his forties or fifties. Maybe even older. But his extravagant look made him appear younger. His sharp features were highlighted by crystal blue eyes that hinted at the marks of time. But he also had the broken face of a gangster and a vicious smile.

I didn't trust him one bit. I politely smiled back and focused my attention on the small party that had just entered the bar. It was composed of two men and two women wearing Stetsons. They were dressed as Texans. I wrote down their order in my notebook and then went straight to the kitchen to give it to Pacho. As I was waiting for the dishes to be ready, I heard Mack's voice over the catcalls directed at the striper.

"Are you shocked?" Mack asked.

Puzzled, I looked at him. "What are you talking about?"

"I'm talking about the girls' behavior around here."

I gave a quick look around me, but Ash had disappeared. He was probably in the company of a woman. The blond stuck to Mack since the beginning of the evening wasn't there anymore.

Before I could open my mouth, he burst out laughing. "You'll get used to it," he told me jokingly.

"Don't be so sure."

"You are now in our world. You need to follow the rules."

Was I dreaming, or was that a threat? Whatever he meant, there was some truth to it.

"I am fine with it," I said. "But I can't say I will follow them blindly."

His large jaw, covered by a blond beard, broke into a smile. I knew he was fooling around.

"I wasn't expecting less from you," Mack said.

Without adding another word, he walked back to the big table where seven or eight men wearing Wild Crows leather jackets were sitting.

"Mack is a wicked kid," Mona whispered in my ear,

startling me at the same time. "A handsome bad kid, but still a bad kid."

Shooting me a knowing smile, she left to attend to another customer at the other end of the bar. It was a lot to take in, and that man's malicious eyes made me suspicious of him. He was a player. I could sense it. He thrived on taking challenges and being provocative. I would stake my life on it. I was not ready to be another trophy in his collection. Pacho called me out. The tacos and the burger were waiting for me in the serving hatch. I hurried to bring them to the customers, who were getting impatient.

8

JERRY

Bigma couldn't help himself. Once again, that idiot had gotten into trouble, and the club had to take care of it. Nevertheless, he was a good man. He was loyal and courageous, and he knew the meaning of brotherhood. It was running through his veins. But his temper was always getting in the way. When he was crossed, he immediately lost his temper. He and Hanger were just back from Reno, where I had sent them to meet Suerte Ramirez, the Bandoleros' leader. The Bandoleros was the most influential club in Nevada. Among its members, there was Franck Bogart, alias Frankie, who was an old friend of mine. He presided over the Wild Crows on the other side of the state line. We always knew our plan was risky. Taking away the lucrative arms trafficking business from the Russians seemed complicated, but it was worth it. If we managed to strike a deal with the Bandoleros, the club's benefits would triple.

In theory, it should have gone like clockwork. Just a quick trip to talk about business, that was all. The problem was that Bigma never played by the rules. I should probably have sent Ash instead of him. He was more mature and more stable. I wanted to give Bigma a chance to prove he could keep control and strike a good business deal. What a stupid mistake!

Now, we had one huge problem on our hands. Another thing to deal with. If this lifestyle gave me the freedom I needed, it also meant assuming overwhelming responsibilities sometimes. And no one, absolutely no one, could imagine what it was like unless they presided over a motorcycle club themselves. One day, I would step down to heal my old carcass. But that moment had not come yet. It was the opposite.

We had an emergency that needed to be taken care of. Once again, Bigma had messed everything up. After successful negotiations, my men spotted one of the Kasabov brother's cars, which was parked not far from the shed where the meeting had taken place. They immediately thought they had fallen into a trap.

They should have laid low until we had a chance to discuss the situation. That was what Hanger had suggested to him, but instead, Bigma had decided to get out and talk to the Russians. He had taunted and questioned Kasabov about his presence in the neighborhood. But the Russians' sense of humor was limited when it came to being screwed by another gang. There had been a dangerous car chase between a Jeep and two Harleys in the streets of Reno, which had attracted attention to our little business.

A few gunshots were exchanged, but fortunately, no one had been hurt. It could have been worse. But sooner or later, the Kasabovs would retaliate. They probably had a fair idea of our plan, and I could tell they didn't appreciate it. We were about to challenge them on their primary source of income. They would not accept it. It was risky. Blood would flow, but it was necessary.

I had no choice. The workshop and the bar didn't generate enough cash to finance our club. We had given up selling cocaine a few years back, and the occasional contracts we were getting for our girls would not be enough to get back on our feet. Besides, we were still dealing weapons on the West Coast, and Reno was the place to be. The war was getting more intense each day, and the competition was inevitable. If I didn't take action, the club was done, and I couldn't accept it. Many men had given their lives for the club. It was so much more than a few roaring engines run by bikers sharing their passion. We were a family, and each member worked for the community. It gave us the opportunity to live as outlaws. The danger was part of our lives, but it was our choice. We were children of the wind.

I crushed my cigarette in the ashtray before slapping Bigma on the back. Marcus Flint was his real name. He got his nickname from his muscular body and his dark skin. I couldn't remember exactly which one of my men gave it to him. Many of us had one, and most of the time, they referred to a physical trait or an action done in the name of the club. Bigma grumbled but stayed silent. He was aware he had messed up.

"You're pissing me off, Big."

"Sorry, boss. But this asshole was following us."

"One more reason not to make things worse."

"Our cover was blown," Hanger objected.

I looked at him. The two men had been as thick as thieves for more than three years when Hanger was accepted as one of ours after a trial period of several months.

"We mustn't let our guard down. They will probably come around soon. Pass the word around," I ordered Bigma in an icy tone.

He nodded and walked back to the bar while the evening breeze brushed against our faces.

I looked at Hanger. "Stay alert tonight. Messing around with the Russians is never without conse-quences."

"Same with us," he said with a smirk.

Defeated, I breathed out. "Get the fuck out of here."

When he finally left, I enjoyed a few moments of soli-tude. I lit up another cigarette and reflected on my day. And what a day! In the morning, Casey had come to my office to tell me he wanted to leave us and live a nomadic life for a year or two. He wanted to see the world. How could I blame him? Casey had just turned twenty-two. I sighed as I would have liked him to stay.

Then, Joe had entered my life unexpectedly. A kid

who rekindled a past I had forgotten. It was like being kicked in the ass and yanked back thirty years.

Maggie Blake.

Our story had been short and intense.

We were young, deeply in love, and careless like young people who didn't give a damn about the future. I had been dreaming for three years, thinking I had found the woman who would share my life. I already belonged to the club, having joined when it was founded in 1975.

Maggie had moved to Sacramento to take part in a music band that needed her angelic voice to record an album. Our paths had crossed, and the relationship that ensued had been unforgettable and explosive. I had never been moved like that by a woman. Thinking about her sweet face, a smile came to mine. Maggie looked like an angel, but I belonged to a world filled with brutes. It couldn't last. And it didn't. Now, this kid was bringing back all these memories buried in my brain. I couldn't blame her. She wanted to know the truth, but I didn't need this.

A clueless man is a happy one, but I couldn't turn a blind eye. I had to deal with what life had in store for me. Good or bad, time would tell. *Damn it, Maggie. Why did you hide this kid and the truth for so many years?* But I could quickly figure out why. I wasn't an ideal father. I wouldn't have been able to give her a decent life or something close to a normal one if one could define normal. Anyway, Maggie wouldn't have been able to adapt to my lifestyle.

Now, Mona and our son had found their place in the club. Casey's childhood had not been unhappier than any other kid's. It had been different, but was it that bad? This difference made his life meaningful. The three of us loved each other very much. Better than that, we were also part of a bigger family, The Wild Crows. It was a true brotherhood. We were all loyal and ready to do whatever it took to help one another. How many people could say they had that in their lives? Of course, we didn't fit in. So what? Our life was divergent, but for god's sake, we were enjoying every moment of it. A short and fulfilled life was worth thousands, filled with endless boredom.

So, we had to deal with this kid. Joe. Josephine. Convinced that her mother named her after the famous Miss Baker, I laughed. She had always been artistic. My responsibility was to teach my daughter how things worked around here. A mistake could be costly. But first of all, I had to be sure I had made myself clear to the guys. I wouldn't tolerate any inappropriate behavior. Joe was twenty-seven, but she didn't know who she was dealing with. I did. I loved my brothers, but I was aware of their low instincts. I didn't want my daughter — god, it felt so strange to pronounce this word — to be subjected to their uncontrollable libido and their gangsta attitude.

If she wanted to stay, she would need some time to adapt. I realized that. The gap between her world and ours was so broad it would be a challenge for her. It would be an overwhelming step to take. And after taking it, it would be impossible to go back. But she wouldn't be alone. I was hoping she would choose to stay with me. I would do anything for this to happen. At least Mona had taken the news rather well. Casey would be informed after his return from San Francisco in a few days. I didn't know what his reaction would be. He had a hot temper, and it could flare up in a second. After all, I had done nothing wrong. Joe was a part of a past that had reappeared unexpectedly.

I crushed my cigarette in the ashtray and decided to go back inside. Before sitting at the table with my men, I walked to the counter to make sure my new waitress was doing fine.

"How is it going?" I asked Joe.

She gave me a surprised look and smiled. How could I not be under the charm of her doll-like face? Her beautiful green eyes shone under her black bangs. *I'd better talk to the members of the club again.*

"I'm fine," she said.

She was hanging on. She hadn't left, even after meeting the sweeties and the dancers. It was my first victory. There would be many more battles to fight before I could be sure she would stay. I grabbed my lovely little wife by the waist and kissed her neck. Surprised, she squealed. She slapped me on the shoulder, and we laughed.

"You're bad," she reprimanded me with a false pout on her goddess lips.

I flashed my teeth like a predator ready to bite and leaned toward her ear. "Thanks for taking care of her," I whispered.

"You're welcome."

We looked at each other for a few seconds. It was an intense moment, lost in the ocean of time.

I joined my crew at the table. The stripers left the stage under the customers' howls and applause. Then,

Johnny Conrad took over with his guitar and his famous hat. The former Marine began his show by playing the most famous folk songs he usually played every Saturday night. Mona brought another round of beer, and I winked at her. Ash and Laz raised their glasses, and we cheered, enjoying being part of this family. Our family.

9

JOE

Since waking up, my headache had only worsened. Despite sleeping late, I still felt exhausted. Mona had told me to be at the Devil's Trip by 6:00 p.m., leaving me the morning to rest and the afternoon for errands—just one, really. The only reason I was here was my father.

The strong coffee I had just downed gave me a moment of clarity, shaking off the last bit of grogginess. After a hot shower, I decided to drive into town to stock up on groceries. My fridge was empty, and my stomach was already protesting.

I left the apartment, enjoying the soft kiss of the sun on my cheeks while a breeze was blowing through my hair. Feeling the pangs of hunger, I ran down the stairs. When I arrived the day before, I had noticed a Walgreens. It was about a few minutes' drive. As I got to my Comet, a familiar voice stopped me in my tracks in the big parking lot.

"Joe! Hi!"

I immediately recognized the rasped and deep voice. Jerry was standing in front of the workshop, and he was waving at me. I smiled as I walked to him. Under his leather jacket bearing the logo of the club, he was wearing a t-shirt stained with motor oil.

"Hi," I replied. "I'm on my way to the grocery store."

Having a chat with the father I had just met the day before wasn't natural at all. I improvised.

"Hey, what would you say if we went for a drive when you come back?" Jerry asked.

I stared at him wide-eyed, probably looking like a little girl who had just been told there was a surprise for her. It was a gift.

I nodded before any word could come out of my mouth. "Yes, of course. It would be my pleasure!"

I quickly waved at Ash and Billy, a white-haired guy who was an early member of the club. Installed on their motorcycles, they seemed lost in their conversation, but they politely waved back at me.

"I won't be long," I explained.

"Take your time. I haven't got anything planned for today."

"No kidding," I joked.

The smile he gave me told me I was right: He had worked things out so he could be available for me. Just for me. I noticed the president's tag which was embroidered on his jacket. He was probably very proud of it.

"See you later, Mr. President," I joked, trying to keep things light.

As I turned around to walk to my car, a brown Jeep with flashing cherry and blue lights drove through the gate. I glanced at Jerry, who was watching his men. Then, he turned his eyes back to me. He seemed concerned, but he smiled at me as if he wanted to reassure me. The car stopped just in front of us, and a woman got out. I recognized the sheriff's star pinned to her brown shirt. She was in her forties, and her ponytail was tucked under her hat. I immediately noticed the gun she was wearing on her belt. I couldn't remember being so close to a deadly weapon. Without a smile, she walked towards Jerry, and I looked at her from where I was standing. Naturally, Ash and Billy got off their bikes and joined us while maintaining a safe distance. The atmosphere got heavy.

"Jerry," she said in a severe tone while extending her hand to him.

My father politely shook it, puzzled by the officer's presence.

"Sheriff Thompson," he said, still shaking her hand. "What can I do for you?"

She greeted me with a simple nod of her head and glanced at the two bikers standing right behind us. "The Reno Police Department contacted me early this morning, Jerry. It seems that two bikers from your crew were spotted during a gunfight yesterday afternoon."

I winced. A gunfight. For real? Did my father have anything to do with it? He had the look of a gangster. His men, too. But it was not a reason to suspect them. They were not ideal romantic partners, but it was a long stretch to consider them as gangsters capable of firing their guns in broad daylight. It was surreal. My father cleared his throat, and he grinned arrogantly. For an instant, I was skeptical. No, it was impossible. I was watching his lips, but the sheriff spoke first.

"Sorry, but who are you?" she asked.

I suddenly realized she was talking to me.

"A customer," my father replied. "She's having some problems with her Comet. Nothing serious. These damned cars look good, but they need to be serviced correctly. Otherwise, they break down."

I went along with his lie, guessing he was trying to protect me. But from what? The sheriff looked at me carefully before coming to the conclusion I was not the person she was looking for.

"And about yesterday, do you have anything to add, Jerry?"

She had already forgotten about me and had walked straight to my father. Even with a supposed customer hanging around, she didn't beat around the bush... or it was a clever trick to pressure Jerry and his men.

"I don't know anything," he replied assuredly.

She looked at him silently for a few seconds. "Well," she said, wincing slightly. "Hard to believe, as our witness clearly identified the jackets bearing the logo of your club ..."

"Well, I can only think of two things. Either your witness is short-sighted, or he wants us to take the blame. We have a lot of enemies, as you know."

The sheriff laughed. "No kidding."

My father chuckled, which made him cough a little.

She was outspoken, and he seemed to be amused. On this point, they were made of the same cloth.

"Fine," she said. "If you hear about anything, you'd better let me know."

"You can count on me, Sheriff," my father replied.

Both the Sheriff and I gave him an irritated look. Why was he behaving like this in front of a representative of the law? He was playing with fire, and he seemed to enjoy it. I didn't like that.

"Gentlemen..."

The sheriff looked carefully at each man before returning to her Jeep. She was visibly annoyed by my father's silence. Just before she drove off, she rolled down her window so she could speak to them one last time.

"Jerry, don't you get it? The day the shit hits the fan, it would be wise to have me on your side... don't be a fool! You and I have everything to lose. We both want the best for Monty Valley. I know we see things differently, but it's up to you to cooperate with us."

Then, we heard the roaring engine sound and screeching of tires as she drove away. Ash took a sigh of relief.

"What was that?" I asked.

My father winced, apparently embarrassed by my question.

"This..." he said, looking over my shoulder, "...was a typical day at the club. You'll get used to it."

He seemed so confident. He had to be for both of us. Maybe it was better like this. I was so puzzled by recent events. The two men finally came to us.

"We had it coming," said Billy.

"Yup," Jerry grumbled. He looked at me briefly. "I guess you have questions to ask me. We'll talk when you come back."

I guessed it was his way of putting an end to the discussion. But I wasn't going to let him get away with it. If he wanted me to be part of his life, I needed to know. It wouldn't budge.

"Okay," I said. "Later."

The next second, he was already walking back to his small office in the workshop. I saw him hit a pile of papers while mumbling to himself. He had tried to look innocent, but the sheriff's visit had upset him. I was asking myself where I had landed when I decided to visit this father I was longing to meet.

Ash's rasping voice brought me back to reality. "Last night, I told you we would explain the club's rules. It starts now, Sweetheart. Rule number one: the less you know, the safer you are."

I looked at him, intrigued by his words.

"Rule number two," he said. "If it smells like shit, if it looks like shit, then it is shit. Stay away from it. Don't ask too many questions. And you're back to rule number one."

Apart from his intense blue eyes, nothing indicated I could trust him. His face's sharp features made him look like a brute, and his messy dark locks made me think of a lunatic. He was looking at me so intently that I started to feel uneasy. Then, I realized he was waiting for a sign that would tell him I understood.

"Got it," I said

I was lying, but I would deal with it later. Ash seemed relieved, and Billy came to his rescue.

"It's for your own good, Joe," Billy said. "Here, women stay out of our business."

"Fine," I said bitterly. "But I didn't cross the state line to hear this. I'll let you take care of this bullshit."

I turned around, still upset and scared to death. But I had to face the truth. The Wild Crows were not just motorbike aficionados. Now, I was sure of it. I just needed to know what my father was ready to share with me and how truthful he would be to ensure I would stay by his side. I would find out soon enough.

Stonebridge was not a big town, but in comparison, Monty Valley was a village. You could tell by what was available for sale in the small convenience store. One couldn't be too picky. Nevertheless, I filled up my basket. When I paid at the counter, I was pleased to discover one of the financial benefits of living far from the main highway was cheaper prices. As I said goodbye to the cashier, I heard a voice talking to me.

"Are you exploring the neighborhood?" a male voice asked.

I turned and saw Mack on his bike, helmet on, a mischievous smile lighting up his blond beard. This guy was so cliché. Like a magazine cover—dangerous eyes, model face, arrogant smirk.

Still, I stayed composed.

"Yes," I replied with a smile. "I'm exploring the neighborhood."

He beamed. "Hi."

I smiled again. "Hi."

He lit a cigarette, and I wondered if he could ride and smoke at the same time.

"Are you working tonight, Jerry's Daughter?"

This new nickname made me laugh. I had so many these days.

"Yes."

"Perfect! I'll see you later."

The tattooed blond guy winked at me and gave me another smile. Then, I got the answer to my stupid question as he turned on the engine of his Harley Davidson, holding a cigarette in his hand. With one hand, he lowered his glasses on his eyes and drove into the horizon. A few minutes later, his silhouette melted into the endless straight line that stretched in the distance.

I went back to my old Comet and put my groceries into the trunk. I had to see my father and make him talk. If he wanted me to stay, I needed answers.

10

JOE

I met my father at the beginning of the afternoon. He was still at the workshop, talking with two members of the club I had seen last night, but I hadn't been introduced to them. One was a big, heavily built man with dark skin, and the other one must have been in his sixties or even older. I was surprised one could drive such a heavy bike at that age. Apparently, I was wrong. I greeted them, and they answered me politely. My father interrupted his conversation and walked to me.

"I am sorry, Joe. Something just came up. Nothing serious, but our special time together will have to wait."

I tried to hide my disappointment. My brain was filled with questions concerning that morning's events and the sudden emergency. Again, I would have to wait to get some answers, but my father would not get away with silence.

I nodded. "Too bad. What a pity! I guess we'll do it later. But you and I really need to talk..."

With an amused smile on his face, he acknowledged my words. "You bet." He looked at me for a moment and lifted his arm to signal to the two guys the discussion was over. "Bigma, Lazar, let's go!"

His loud voice startled me. That was another thing I would have to get used to. My father was not a sweet and delicate man.

I helplessly watched them walk away. I left the shed and listened to the sound of the three engines roaring in unison. The trio slowly paraded in front of me. As they were driving, my father waved and smiled at me. His black helmet covered his gray locks, and his eyes were dissimulated behind black sunglasses. They were green like mine. I had noticed this detail. To me, it was undeniable proof that we shared the same DNA.

I returned to the Devil's Trip at 6.00 p.m., as we had agreed on the previous day. Mona was already waiting for me. She was stocking up the fridges for the night. It would be crowded again, but I had gained confidence.

"Hi there," my stepmom said quietly.

"Hi," I said with a smile.

"Ready for tonight?"

"Yeah. Have you seen Jerry?"

Mona winced. "Not since this morning, why?"

"Just asking. We were supposed to spend the afternoon together, but something came up."

"It happens around here, you know."

"I guess I'll get used to it... and to the rest." I sighed.

Mona stopped in her tracks and wrapped her arms around her waist. She had a sad look on her face. "I know what you mean, but you've only been here for a day. It ain't easy. You came unexpectedly, and we are glad you did. You will find your place. It takes time, that's all. Be patient. I told you yesterday everything here is totally different from what you've known so far. You need time to adapt. It's natural."

"You're probably right," I said pensively.

She smiled sweetly at me, and for a few seconds, I couldn't look away. It was surreal how easily she had accepted me into her life. I was grateful for that.

"The sheriff came this morning," I told her, hoping I would get some information.

Mona raised an eyebrow and pretended she didn't know. "It happens."

"Often?"

"Regularly."

"Because of the club's activities?"

She looked at me pensively, probably trying to guess what I had in mind. But it was simple. I just wanted to understand what I would have to deal with.

"The less you know, the better it is," she said.

I had already heard these words earlier in the morning. What were they all hiding? Apparently, I was not supposed to ask questions or get answers. Their shady business had nothing to do with me. Maybe it was better like that. But curiosity was eating me up.

I decided to be patient. Sooner or later, I would know. After all, I had only been here for twenty-four hours. Given the way things were playing out, I was lucky. My father had accepted me. It was the most important thing.

As I was talking with Mona, Jerry came in with Mack and Hanger on his heels. They behaved like a pack of wolves. They were rarely by themselves. He stopped in front of us and swiftly kissed his wife's cheek. I looked at them, moved by the love you could feel between them. Despite his looks, I was sure that Jerry was a devoted husband. He gave me a smile that made me melt.

"Tomorrow," he said, "I'll make some time."

I thanked him with a nod of the head and locked my eyes on his. He was my father. I kept repeating these words to myself, but they still didn't ring true.

"If someone asks for me, I'm upstairs," he whispered to his wife before walking away.

Mack and Hanger each took a place on stools, facing us, and a mischievous smile appeared on the blond and tattooed man's lips. He looked like a Viking. Proud, intimidating, and dangerous.

"Hi again, Junior," he said.

With my eyes wide, I answered. "How many nicknames are you going to give me?"

"As many as I can find."

"Be careful," Mona warned me with a knowing smile.

"Pushing women to the limit is his secret weapon to bed them."

Without protesting, the arrogant womanizer laughed out loud.

"Thanks for helping me out, Mona," he joked.

Playing along, she gave him a broad smile. They had probably known each other for many years. He was ten or fifteen years younger than her.

"You're welcome, love," Mona said. "And leave the kid alone. She deserves better than an old, hungry wolf like you."

"How nice!" I exclaimed. I was now the one laughing. "Mona, I just turned twenty-seven. I am no longer a kid. I can take care of myself. But thanks for your help."

Wanting to show her how grateful I was, I spoke as softly as I could. She seemed happy. I wasn't a tactful person, but I felt she was touched.

"Better safe than sorry. I know Mack."

"Jerry has already warned them. He said the words *tear your balls* and *teeth* in the same sentence."

Mona laughed. "Jerry likes to be heard loud and clear."

"He couldn't have been more explicit," I replied.

"Maybe," she added, glancing at the sexy blond guy.

Mack tried to play the innocent guy by raising his hands in the air.

Mona had to leave us to take an order in the back of the room. I saw one of the dancers coming into the bar. This time, she was dressed in torn skinny jeans and a grunge t-shirt. Her red hair was tied in a ponytail. Carrying a small backpack, she greeted Mack by kissing him on the cheek, then she smiled at me and said, "Hi."

I answered politely and watched her go backstage.

"She seems nice," I said, observing her from the corner of my eye.

"Yep, Jayla is cool," Mack said. "Everyone is around here, at least as long as people play by the rules."

"I still can't believe how easily you, guys, accepted me."

His piercing eyes were locked on mine, and he wasn't smiling anymore. "All of us know how to adapt quickly. Each day brings something new. Yesterday, you were the surprise."

His words brought a smile to my lips.

"And a good one," he added.

The brute in front of me was flirting with me, and he had no shame in it. He didn't seem to know what shame was. I was facing a man who knew what he wanted and was used to getting it. Unfortunately for him, I couldn't be tamed in a few hours. If he wanted to play that game with me, he'd burn his wings. Ever since my disastrous relationship with Arthur, I couldn't trust men anymore. And one-night stands, I'd tried, but they're not for me. If he thought I'd be easy prey, he was wrong. I willfully ignored his remark and went back to work as if nothing had happened.

Mona brought me two sheets from her notepad filled with orders. She left one for Pacho on the serving hatch. She and I took care of the drinks. When my round of beers was served, Mona took care of the heavily loaded tray. The exercise seemed a bit too hazardous for me at this point, but I made up for it by grabbing the hot plates Pacho was sending out while he was shouting at us from his cooking range. Luckily, I reached the table without dropping anything. The group gathered in the back of the room was made of a dozen men. Most of them were dressed as hunters, and I knew why they had come to the Devil's Trip.

In the dimmed light, the reason appeared on the stage. As I was about to walk away, I felt someone pinching my ass cheeks.

Screaming, I jumped. I wasn't quick enough to unmask the man who'd accosted me. They were all sitting on their chairs, laughing out loud. I winced and decided to get the hell out of there rapidly. Then, it happened again. Furious, I quickly turned around while the audience was still cheering Jayla's solo performance at the pole. This time, the culprit didn't have time to hide. I caught him red-handed as he was going back to his chair. With an arrogant and stupid smile, he froze.

Probably encouraged by the laughs of his companions, he called out to me. "Tell me, Sweetheart, this nice ass of yours is next on stage, right?"

He grabbed my wrist, and I let go of my tray. I wished I could have slapped him in the face, but I was frozen. What was happening to me? I was incapable of moving a finger, and he pulled me closer. Luckily or not, my senses started to come back as he forced me to sit on his knees. I fought him with all the strength I had, but his grip was too strong.

"My mates promised me I could get anything I wanted for my birthday. And I want you naked on stage."

He was stinking of alcohol and stupidity—if the latter had an odor. A smell of grime mixed with sweat was floating around.

"Let me go," I demanded.

At that moment, the crazy hunter's bald head violently banged against the wooden table. I think I even heard the muffled sound of his teeth hitting the table. Dumbfounded, I looked at my attacker, but the room was plunged into darkness for Jayla's show.

"Now you apologize to the young lady, dirty old man," Mack growled.

A large white hand flattened the idiot against the table and kept him there with incredible strength. The naked and tattooed forearm dressed in a club jacket belonged to Mack. On his face, I could see rage. Even if I knew he was there to rescue me, he frightened me. The man didn't say a word, so Mack smashed his head one more time. Surprisingly, no one was paying attention to what was going on. There were a few glances, nothing more. Was it because they knew one couldn't challenge the members of the club without having to deal with the consequences?

"Apologize to the young lady, asshole," Mack grumbled so aggressively I was shaking.

Mortified, I picked up my tray on the tiled floor so I could look away.

"Excuse me," came the muffled response.

The guy could barely articulate, and a trickle of blood was coming through his teeth. Shit. I didn't want things to go that far. I could have taken care of him myself. Or not. Anyway, Mack's reaction seemed disproportionate. Speechless, I clutched my jaw. My tall blond savior finally let him go, but he wasn't done. He gave that idiot a heavy slap on the neck to intimidate the man's friends.

"Next time you lay your hands on one of our girls,"

Mack announced. "You'll have to deal with all of us. Do you get it?"

"Yes," mumbled the guy, his face red with shame and fear.

I left hurriedly to meet Mona behind the counter. She was waiting for me with her arms crossed over her chest. Apparently, she had watched Mack's performance.

"Are you okay?" Mona asked.

"Yes," I answered dryly.

I instinctively wiped my hands on my jeans, trying to erase any trace of this guy on me. When I felt someone brush against me, I jumped, frightened it would happen all over again. Then, I recognized the smell of leather and felt Mack's touch on my back. He had just pulled me away from the clutches of an enemy only to keep me closer to him.

"See," he said, "it helps to have someone who keeps an eye on you."

His breath was a whisper against my neck—warm, laced with vice and unspoken expectations. A shiver ran through me before I could stop it.

I met his gaze, searching for answers, but my thoughts were still tangled in the moment, unsure of what to make of it.

Behind me, Mona's voice cut through the silence, "Thank you for protecting her."

I wasn't sure whether I felt saved or just caught in something I didn't yet understand.

11

Joe

I came back, exhausted from the events of the previous night. I was lucky my father could provide me with accommodation on the spot. Driving would have been too risky. I could barely keep my eyes open after we had cleaned up the place. I had wisely decided to stay away from Mack for the rest of the evening, as I didn't know what to think about his intervention. He certainly had got me out of trouble, and it made me discover another side of his personality. I had seen such a brutal look in his cold blue eyes...I had seen rage distort his delicate features.

An angry mask had replaced the natural beauty of his face. I had been accepted into their group so quickly that I sometimes forgot I had been there for less than two days. I didn't know these men. No more Mack than the others. I knew nothing about them, their lives, their vice, or their habits. I had somewhat understood that the club was involved in illegal activities, but I didn't know what they were. It wasn't surprising. It was not a topic you could discuss out loud. Even if I was Jerry's daughter, it didn't mean they would trust me instantly. However, all the members of the club were making sure I was alright. I could feel safe... or not.

The next morning, I wasn't drawn out of bed by the rays of the sun but by a fist banging heavily on my door. I quickly checked the time on my smartphone. It was almost noon. I had almost slept half the day. In slow motion, I walked into the corridor and opened the door. I was only wearing an oversized t-shirt, but I was too sleepy to care about being presentable for my visitor.

Standing in the doorway and wearing sunglasses over his eyes, Jerry was smiling warmly. I tried to mimic him.

"Hello, Miss Sleeping Late," he greeted me.

Puzzled, I cocked my head. "What is it with nicknames around here?"

Amused, my father shook his head. "I don't see what you mean."

"I am sure you do!"

"I can assure you I don't."

"Then stop making one up every day!"

He chuckled. I walked into the kitchen and called out to him, unaware that he was right behind me.

"Coffee?" I asked.

"Yes, please."

Finally, we agreed on something.

The black nectar worked. I came out of my lethargic state, and my eyes were now wide open. "Sorry," I said. "It's been a long time since I worked in a bar."

My father raised his hand. "Don't worry about it."

"I was actually going to come and see you later," I added.

"Billy needs me this afternoon, so I thought I would drop by earlier. If it doesn't work for you, we can always do it another time. There's no hurry."

"Oh, no! That's fine. I agree we're not in a hurry, but I didn't cross the state line to find out about the Devil's Trip," I joked half-heartedly.

Seemingly happy to be spending time with me, Jerry smiled. He drank his hot coffee straight down as I looked at him with admiration. If I did the same, I would probably be burnt to the second or third degree.

"I give you five minutes to get ready. I'll be waiting for you downstairs," he finally said.

"Where are we going?"

"It's a surprise."

"Am I supposed to wear anything...special?"

He looked at me quizzically and winced. "No skirt or high heels."

"Fine. I didn't bring any."

Jerry laughed, and he left my apartment, waving at me. "You remind me of your mom!"

A spontaneous smile came to my lips when I was reminded of her sweet face and her hot temper. Lost in my memories, I started to get ready.

Instead of the five minutes my father had given me, it took me ten or fifteen to join him because of my legendary slow pace in the morning. I locked the door of my new home and put on my sunglasses to protect my eyes, blinded by the early rays of the sun. Well, it was not that early. I went down the three flights of stairs and saw Jerry waiting next to his bike in the parking lot. All the motorcycles, parked in a perfect line, were almost identical with their black paint and their chrome engines. American elegance at its best. My heart skipped a beat. I hesitantly walked to him.

"Are we going for a ride?" I asked.

"You bet!" he told me, smiling widely.

"I never have ridden before."

"There's a first time to everything!" he joked, handing me a half helmet.

I grabbed it and carefully placed it on my head.

"And it's not a bike. It's a Harley," he corrected me.

"Yes, boss."

"Come on!"

I felt a mix of fear and excitement, so I laughed out loud, trying to relax. Jerry sat higher on the bike's seat, and I clumsily lifted my foot above the damned engine. After a few tries, I finally managed to find a comfortable position, and I placed my legs correctly. Then, I heard its distinctive roar, which sounded like a hoarse whisper. Its mechanical melody was invigorating, and I listened to it as I started the engine. Instinctively, I gripped the back of my seat, trying to push away my fear. I'd always been afraid of these machines because of their speed and the accidents they caused. How many had I seen when I worked in the ER? Too many. Between the falls and the burns from the exhaust pipes...

Now, things were different. I was with this father I had met two days earlier, and I had stepped into a brand-new world. We took a small road, and I laughed like a child when the bike drove through a hole in the asphalt. I heard my father laughing as well. Probably sensing my fear, he drove slowly, almost at a walking pace, and we cruised across Monty Valley, enjoying the warm temperature of the day.

I turned my head to the right and looked at the small convenience store where I had shopped the day before and the neighboring park. Straight ahead of us, there was a sign indicating we were about to cross the city limit.

"Are you okay?" shouted Jerry so I could hear him.

"I'm great!" I reassured him, feeling strangely euphoric.

"So, let's go!"

As soon as we had crossed the city limit, he sped off, which caused me to be propelled backward. I screamed out of fear and tightened my grip around his waist. Then, I burst out laughing. The air was blowing in my face.

I closed my eyes and enjoyed the feeling of freedom. It was absolute freedom, unconditional, fleeting, but incredibly intoxicating. The unknown was calling out to me, and I loved it. I couldn't hold back the smile illuminating my face. I didn't think of anything and abandoned myself to that moment. When Jerry started to drive faster, I didn't shiver.

The road line was endless, and I felt like I was flying. I had never felt so relaxed or empty. My hair was whipping my face, and I couldn't stop laughing. Bravely, I let go of my father's jacket. Nervous but galvanized by the intensity of the ride, I slowly opened my hands and fully extended my arms, which were fending the air in a symbolic gesture of confidence.

I wasn't afraid anymore. My fear had disappeared to give way to a desire to feel alive again. I even thought that some of the sorrow that had been crushing my heart for the past two weeks had also gone away. It was still within me, but it was giving me a break, a fleeting instant of carelessness. Getting close to my father helped me accept I had to let go of my mother's soul peacefully.

On this motorbike, which was driving fast on a California highway, everything seemed more bearable, and my young shoulders felt stronger. Freed from my chains, I was flying above all the stress and the pain. Nothing mattered anymore. I was only experiencing this strange communion with myself, with the woman I was deep inside, who I had forgotten along the way. I was reborn, vibrant, happy, and full of hope. I was his daughter. His blood was running through my veins despite the twenty-seven years I had spent away from him.

The passing landscape began to slow down, as well as our speed. Curious, I grabbed my father again and looked around. We were in the middle of nowhere. There were great empty plains and wilderness all around us. Then, we arrived at a crossroads, which was not indicated by any road sign. One needed to be familiar with the place so as not to miss it.

Jerry turned right, and instinctively, my body followed the motorcycle's angle. The narrow road gradually became a dirt road. I had no idea what was waiting for us at the end of it. On the contrary, he seemed to know precisely what he was doing. I could tell he knew this place well. A few minutes later, he parked his bike on the shoulder of the road and turned off the engine. The silence troubled me. Surprisingly, I had enjoyed the roaring sound of the Harley on the way, and even got used to it. It was soothing.

"We've arrived," my father said as he removed his helmet from his head.

I looked around. We were surrounded by sparse yellowish tall grass and moon-like sandy patches, which made the landscape look somewhat hostile.

"You can get off," he told me.

I did and released my tangled hair from under the helmet. "Where are we exactly?"

"Come on," he said mischievously.

Curious, I followed him. We walked a few feet, and then I saw it. Behind a large bank was a small boardwalk. That small path, hidden like a treasure of nature, excited my curiosity. A few more steps gave me the answer I was looking for. We walked over a small mound, and just behind it, I discovered a breathtaking sight. A wild and peaceful lake that reminded me of the indomitable person-ality of my father. It was like a haven of peace, completely isolated from the rest of the world. Just a few birds were disturbing the surrounding silence.

"It's gorgeous," I marveled.

"Yes," he just answered.

He waved, inviting me to follow him on a path that bordered the lake. A little bit further along, a few trees were gathered as if they stayed close to each other so they wouldn't be lost in the endless plains and dunes around them. This was our destination. I was surprised to see a small woodshed along the way. Jerry asked me to wait for him for a few minutes, and he walked to a place that looked like a shop. A few minutes later, he came back with a paper bag in his hand and a broad smile on his face.

We sat on the yellowish grass under the big pines. Like a child, I gave him a mischievous look. He had planned a picnic, and I couldn't be happier. I chose one of the sandwiches and gave him the other one. Nature became our anchor point, as we were having an out-of-time experience. It bonded us in a way that words were no more necessary to express our feelings. Glancing at each other between two bites, we were smiling heartily. One could feel pure happiness floating around.

A father and his daughter finally reunited. I decided not to break this magic moment and kept to myself all the questions I was burning to ask. We finished our meal in bliss. Then, I felt something that was entirely new to me. He protectively put his arm dressed in the leather jacket around my shoulders, and I melted. We looked at each other for a long time, and I put my head on his shoulder.

"What about a short walk?" he asked.

I enjoyed this bond I had missed for so many years, the

smell of his jacket, and the feeling of being totally safe when I was in his arms. I cocked my head and smiled at him. We quietly continued our walk around the lake. I guess both of us were afraid to see this fleeting moment– our moment- come to an end. Life had given us a gift, and we wanted to fully enjoy it.

When a majestic white heron flew over our heads, I ducked, and my father made fun of me. We laughed together, and it felt good...so good. But I thought it was time for me to get answers. I had to know who I was dealing with. Maybe I was going to spoil this idyllic moment, but if I wanted to live around him, I needed to know.

I gathered my courage and took the leap. "Can I ask you something?"

As if he was expecting it, Jerry threw his head back-ward. Then he opened his mouth, looking like he was smiling at the sky. With his eyes locked on me, he kept walking, and I could almost see his stare behind his black sunglasses.

"I wasn't expecting less from you," he said.

I tried to put on my sweetest face as a way to apologize for the questions I was about to ask. "It's just that... I need to know you. Well, I mean, I need to get to know you."

"I get it. What do you want to know exactly? Fire away."

"Will you tell me the whole truth?"

"The whole truth. I promise."

I sighed.

"What is exactly this club of yours?" I asked.

I was blunt, but this question had been eating me up

since the sheriff's visit. I wouldn't be able to trust him like I was supposed to if I didn't know the whole truth. For the first time since I arrived, my father seemed less confident.

"The Wild Crows Club was founded in 1975 by Ron Bagwell. At that time, we were only five or six members. We loved motorcycles, and this passion was our bond. We thought we should create a club. Some had already popped up in other towns. We saw it as a way to escape the routine and live off our passion and other things."

I didn't expect this kind of answer. His smile was full of regrets.

"This Ron Bagwell is he... dead?"

Jerry lowered his head, and he was scraping off the ground with his shoe. I noticed we had stopped walking.

"Yes, sweetheart. He died a few years ago."

Putting on a brave mask, my father took a deep breath. He was probably too proud to let his pain show, but I could see it in the way his mouth was distorted when he tried to smile. I respected his modesty and said nothing.

"I am sorry," I said. "And what are these other things?"

I had to know. I didn't want to remind him of the painful deaths of some of the original members of the club, but I would get my answers. Once again, I felt he was embarrassed by my question. He coughed, and I understood he was looking for an acceptable solution. What could be so bad? I started to worry.

"Daddy," I said. Hearing this word for the first time made my father flinch. "You promised you would tell me the whole truth. Yesterday, the sheriff came to tell you that some of your men had been seen in a gunfight in Reno. Is that true?"

He winced, and then he puffed. I was annoying him, or my questions were.

"Listen, Joe," he began hesitantly. "Whatever happens in the club, the less you know about it, the safer it is, do you understand?"

His voice became softer, and I wondered. What were exactly the risks?

"I don't know what you're talking about... And you said you'd tell the whole truth," I reminded him.

After looking at each other silently for a few seconds, he capitulated. At least partially. "The club needs money, and we have chosen to live like outcasts. We need to find ways to get by."

"Don't justify yourself, Daddy. I just want to know what's going on. If I stay with you, I need to know... do you...sell drugs?"

I didn't really care about the answer as long as I knew the truth. After the sheriff's visit and their silence, I knew they were not model citizens. They were all involved in some shady business, and I was not there to judge them.

"No," my father finally answered. "We stopped dealing drugs years ago. It was too dangerous. Too many gangs on the market. Not to mention that some of our guys couldn't stay clean. It was a damned mess..."

Once again, he seemed lost in his memories for a few seconds. In the meantime, I was processing the information. So, they had sold illicit drugs before.

"Then what? I said impatiently. Heists? Robberies?"

"No."

"Tell me, please. Not knowing is the worst."

"Weapons," he said in an annoyed tone.

"What did you say? ... weapons?" I mumbled.

Alright, I was trying not to be judgmental. The information was slowly sinking in, and I had to compose my face in front of my gangster father.

"We take delivery and sell them. Now, you know everything."

It was a forced confession, and he resented it. I could feel his anger.

"Thanks," I whispered.

Puzzled, he looked at me for a second.

"I'm telling you we sell arms, and you thank me?"

I laughed involuntarily. His overprotective instincts were so touching that I couldn't resist.

"I am grateful you told me the whole truth. You only met me a few days ago. It was risky. I could have taken advantage of you, you know."

I meant every word. How could he be sure I was not an undercover ATF agent pretending to be his daughter? It would have been possible. But I was his legitimate child, eager to know who he really was under his leather jacket and his pride. I knew I'd have to scratch the surface to achieve this.

Amused, he breathed out. "You're the spitting image of your mom."

"I'm not. She was blond." I answered.

"You have her smile, and you look at me like she used to."

His words were full of emotion. I was overwhelmed.

"I've just found out I have a daughter," he whispered. "And I have every intention to do whatever it takes for her to stay with me."

I swallowed hard. Jerry pulled back his sunglasses on his eyes as if they protected his modesty. I assumed he was also feeling the same sudden wave of affection. We still didn't know each other very well, but I had his genes. He was part of me, and even if life had played a trick on us, that would never change. I didn't need more time to get used to this idea. It felt natural to me. I had always been his daughter, and our meeting for the first time made it real.

12

JERRY

I parked my old Harley, along with the others, which were in front of the workshop. It had been a long time since someone sat on the back of my seat. Mona wouldn't ride since she had a bad fall three years ago. Now, I was a lonely rider. Joe got off the bike, and she took her helmet off. I did the same. Then, I turned towards her, trying to figure out my feelings. What was she thinking of me?

I was an old father who was just figuring out how to relate to his daughter. She gave me a smile that was worth all the money in the world. It was so sincere. Despite my confession, she was still there, at least for now. Her wish to bond with me was stronger than the shady parts of my life, at least for the moment. It wouldn't last, but I promised myself to enjoy every moment spent with her.

"Here," she told me, handing me the helmet.

"Keep it. You'll need it later."

Her smile was so sweet.

"Okay. Thanks..."

Her eyes looked over my shoulder toward the shed. Apparently, something had caught her attention.

"It looks like we have a welcoming committee."

I turned around and saw Ash, Mack, and Billy in the distance. I put my arm around my daughter's young shoulders–it was so damned strange to think these words!–We walked towards them. Slumped on a pile of tires, Mack was playing with his knife. His eyes were as sharp as the blade.

He greeted me with a polite "Hi, Boss," but I immediately noticed that his attention was drawn to someone else, Joe.

I glared at him, but he didn't stop. I grunted, and he looked away for a minute. I had known him for years, and he had never changed. He always behaved like this when he saw a pair of breasts. But in this case, we were talking about my daughter and not a sweetie.

She had integrity, and I wanted to make sure it would stay that way. She was a grown-up woman, and I couldn't tell her what to do. However, I would talk to Mack again and ask him to go and play with his dick somewhere else. My first warning had not been clear enough. I would have to do something about it. Joe was not one of these girls. She deserved better than this crazy predator. Ash must have noticed the anger in my eyes because he slapped me hard on the back.

"Hey, Boss, where have you been? I tried to call you at least five times since this morning."

"I turned off my phone," I informed him.

It had been such a great idea. Joe and I had an opportunity to spend time together, far away from the problems of the club and its dangers. My friend didn't ask any more questions.

Ash was a good guy. Among all my fellow brothers in the club, he was undoubtedly one I would put on the short list of guys I would trust with my life. He had joined the club twenty years ago, and I had never regretted letting him in. He was always in control, and I knew I could trust him completely. I sometimes wondered what was going on in his head, as he was difficult and sometimes harsh. However, I appreciated his loyalty and self-sacrifice. He was a strange mix of the mad scientist, Elvis, and the Terminator, topped with a drizzle of whiskey and other vices men like him had.

"What's the emergency?" I asked.

He glanced at Joe, whom I was still holding by the arm so Mack would understand to stay away.

"You can talk freely," I reassured him, tightening my grip.

My daughter let a quick smile pass her lips. Ash nodded and talked. His lips quivered before he could finish his sentence. Why was he so emotional?

"Varozky called."

"Varozky?" I repeated incredulously.

The sleazy lawyer was the only one we could afford to defend Gale, one of our members who had been arrested for acts of violence and possession four years ago. Though he couldn't avoid detention, he got a pretty good deal. Five years instead of ten. Poor old Gale was now behind bars.

"Yeah," Ash confirmed enthusiastically. "Gale will be out tomorrow."

His words hit me like a thunderbolt.

"Fuck!"

That was all I could say at that moment. I even had forgotten about Joe for a moment.

Then, Billy spoke. "He received early release for good conduct."

I wasn't expecting that! It was good news for the club. Billy, with his unruly and frizzy white hair matching his long beard, was smiling childishly. Our eldest member was as happy as I was. Billy had founded this club with Ron. We owed him everything.

"Fuck, that's some good news!" I jubilated.

I let go of Joe, and Ash gave me another hard slap on the back. Billy hugged me. We, the early members, had this capacity to enjoy any positive event. It was one of the few advantages of aging. Mack was smiling absently as he planted his blade into a wooden beam behind him. He jumped from the pile of tires and walked towards Joe. I didn't give him time to put on another show for her.

"Mack, get the word around. We'll have a meeting tonight!"

He inflated his lungs while a hesitating smile appeared on his square jaw. "I am on it, Boss."

Then, he walked away, not without glancing one more time at my beautiful daughter. My eyes followed him as Joe looked away. I'd have to talk with the kid standing next to me about what she could expect from this womanizer. Then, she could do whatever she wanted. I didn't want to lock her up in a gilded cage. I hadn't been there in her early years, so I just wanted to protect her. Even just for a little while. Sooner or later, if she chose to stay with me in Monty Valley, she would inevitably be in harm's way. I was trying to delay that damned moment for as long as I could.

"Who is Gale?" she finally asked.

Her voice was so soft compared to our world's brutality. Once more, I melted.

"One of us," I answered.

We were all gathered around the table Ron had built in 1975 when the club was created. I presided with my hammer in hand. On my left, there was Billy, my right-hand man, Ash, and Bigma, along with Hanger, Mack, Lazar, and Foxy, sat on my right. The latter got his nickname from his bizarre red and frizzy hair. Billy had given it to him. It sounded good, and it stuck.

I slammed my hammer on the table three times to declare the session open. "Thanks for coming, guys."

A few heads nodded, and I carried on. "I asked you to

come tonight because I have something important to share with you."

Playfully, I kept a serious face as I looked at them. They immediately panicked. Given our current problems, a few were undoubtedly wondering why I had gathered them. Looking like an executioner about to strike, I sighed. I saw Bigma impatiently tap his fingers while Lazar was tapping his legs under the table. I smiled widely, realizing my little scheme was working well.

"Gale will be out tomorrow!"

It was such a relief. It was amazing to see how four little words could lighten up the atmosphere in a heartbeat! Billy decided to tell the story while Bigma kept hitting the table with his fist to express his joy.

"What the fuck! You had me there!" laughed Hanger, pointing his finger at me.

"I need volunteers to give him a ride from Stratford," I said.

Ash raised his hand, followed by Hanger.

"I'll take care of it," said Ash.

"I'm in," added Hanger.

"It works for me. Ash, you'll ride. Hang, you'll drive the van."

They both approved my decision. We had our routine for such trips. It was better not to put all your eggs in the same basket, especially with our lifestyle. We had to anticipate.

The office door opened suddenly, and we all froze. The young man with brown hair, standing in the doorway, was wearing the club's jacket.

"Take a chair, Casey," I said. "The guys will tell you

everything at the end of the meeting. Happy to see you, son!"

Smiling at me, he sat between Foxy and Lazar. He was my kid, and he was as beautiful as his mother. As tiresome sometimes! I let out a laugh.

"Tell us," I said. "How did it go in San Francisco?"

He breathed in and shortly told us about his trip. I had sent him there to judge his potential. He was the youngest of the group. If he wanted to earn the other members' respect, he had to prove himself. Being my son didn't give him any special rights, on the contrary. He had to show them what he was made of.

"Yeah. Things got complicated when I arrived. Lionel wasn't expecting me to show up. He thought you'd be there," he informed me.

Lionel Munch was from the old guard. He owned a bunch of nightclubs in town, and we had been in business since forever. We weren't selling drugs anymore, but he was interested in reselling weapons. He was one of our main customers, and he knew it all too well. That's probably why he was expecting all of us to make the trip, and especially myself.

"Lionel is an asshole," I said. "But he is fucking rich. So, we have to keep quiet."

"Yeah. I know, Dad. So, I flattered him to calm him down, and we negotiated."

"And?" I prodded impatiently.

"And I convinced him to double his order."

I could barely breathe. "Are you kidding me?"

Proud as a peacock, the kid stretched like a cat and

crossed his arms behind his head. "I'm not messing around!"

We were all speechless. Suddenly, Hanger grabbed him by the shoulders. His two large hands covered most of his frail chest. Then, he shook him so hard that his arrogant smile disappeared. He could probably have broken his bones with bare hands.

"This kid is priceless!" Hanger said. "I told you!"

Dumbfounded, I dropped into my chair. My son's ego had been dangerously growing lately, and he didn't like it. Still, I had to admit I was impressed. Around the table, my men were euphoric, and Ash hit the wooden surface several times, cheering for my boy.

"Well done," I said uneasily, as everyone had their eyes fixed on me, awaiting my reaction.

When things cooled down, we tackled the difficult topic of the Karabasovs. Luckily, they hadn't contacted us. I hoped we might avoid a dirty war against those crazy Russians. Bigma was waiting to hear from the Bandoleros. So far, there had been no news. I finally put an end to the meeting, feeling we were moving forward. For the past few months, the finances of the club had been low, so I'd asked each member to think about new ways to make money. No serious proposition had been made so far. At least nothing that made sense.

I had refused Hanger's bright idea to prostitute our girls. Sometimes, we would provide one or two girls to an important customer to close a deal. Everybody got something out of it. We gave away a big chunk of the money to the sweetie, our cash register was full, and our customer was satisfied. Yet, I didn't want to keep repeating this pattern. I wasn't a pimp. I didn't have as many choices as I thought I had. I was still hoping we could put the club back on its feet, sooner or later, with as little damage as possible. Stealing some of the Karabasovs' business was one way to achieve our goal, but no one knew the price we would have to pay for it.

The guys finally left the room one by one, and I grabbed Casey by the shoulder. When we were alone, we sat at the table.

"I am proud of you, Son. Seriously. Well done."

He looked at me for a few seconds, seemingly embarrassed.

"Thanks, Dad."

We kept silent and looked at each other. Then, I decided it was time for us to talk about one delicate matter.

"There is a new girl around here."

"I know."

I swallowed hard. "How...do you know?"

"Mom. She's been calling me every day since I left ... You know how she is."

I winced. "I do."

"Is she cool?"

I paused and smiled. "Yeah, she is cool."

13

JOE

My father had given me the night off. On weekdays, business was slow, so he decided it was not necessary to have two waitresses working behind the counter. I took the opportunity to recharge my batteries. I locked myself in my new home and enjoyed a long hot bath. I had to process so many things lately that I needed this moment of solitude and calm. To end a perfect evening, I called Saddie.

Hesitant at first, I finally told her everything. Well, almost everything, to be honest. I voluntarily omitted the discussion I'd had earlier in the afternoon. It was the club's business and nobody else's. She was sincerely happy for me and shrieked as I expected her to do. I talked about the place, which was not very attractive at first sight, and then I told her about the warm welcome I had received from my father and his wife. I also tried to describe the members of the club, even though I didn't know them that well.

When I uttered the word *biker*, my ex-colleague squeaked–literally! That was Saddie–I could tell she was fantasizing about sexy and dangerous fugitives. Mischievously, I ruined her dream by telling her that reality was less glamorous. After chatting away for an hour, we finally hung up, promising each other to call very soon. I missed my friend. Then, Morpheus, the god of dreams, came to greet me in his arms, probably because of the overwhelming emotions of the day. I didn't resist and joined him to enjoy a restful night.

I woke up bright and early, body and soul at peace. I didn't need to be at the Devil's Trip before 4 p.m. From what I had understood, one of the members of the club was getting out of jail that day. I didn't know why he was behind bars, and I must admit I didn't dare to ask. I was told many times that a new girl shouldn't ask questions. I left the complex in the early afternoon, not knowing exactly where I would go.

I decided to drive along the long straight line I had taken with Jerry the previous day and see what was beyond the horizon. With rolled-down windows and my sunglasses covering my eyes, I sped off. It was fun, but not as much as riding on a motorcycle. A dreamy smile came over my face.

As I started to slow down, a strange sound caught my attention. A repeated high-pitched sound. A police siren. Shit! I checked the speedometer. *Whoops.* I grumbled and cursed. Behind me, I saw a police car catching up and flashing its lights. The officer used his loudspeaker to tell me to stop the vehicle on the side of the road, and I obeyed.

A cloud of dust rose through the air when I turned off the engine. Speed had nothing to do with it—the road was dusty and dry. I checked my wing mirror. A guy dressed in a sheriff's uniform was getting out of his car and started walking towards me. I was sure I was screwed. Moving like an arrogant cowboy, he walked to my car and stopped next to my open window.

"Good morning," he said, lifting his sunglasses.

It was so cliché, but I didn't find it amusing. I opted to give him an innocent smile. It sometimes worked, especially with macho men - and I could tell by the way he was looking at me and standing with his legs spread apart that he was a player. I was sure of it. I had a radar to detect these assholes. I decided I would not try to seduce him but keep that option open if I had no other choice.

"Hello," I said politely.

"Do you know what the speed limit is on this road?"

I cleverly pretended to look at my speedometer and

shrugged theatrically. "To tell you the truth, no. I'm not from here. I'm just visiting..."

The officer sighed before answering. I knew the answer, but I pretended I didn't.

"Sixty-five, ma'am."

"Oh," I said as if it was news to me. "I guess I was driving faster than I thought..."

My performance might have won me an Oscar. Or not.

"You're damned right."

I had blown my chance. No career in Hollywood for me.

I looked at his brown uniform. There was no star pinned on it, and I remembered I had met the sheriff the day before. I guessed he was her deputy.

"Do you know what is the penalty for speeding?" he asked.

I guessed it was time to pay for my carelessness. The lecture was about to start. "A fine?"

"A hundred and fifty dollars fine," the officer specified.

"It's a lot of money for a second of inattention," I said tentatively.

He frowned.

"Can I see your driver's license and the papers of the vehicle, please, ma'am?"

I was up to my neck, so I searched in my bag and handed them out my license and registration. He looked at them quickly and asked me to wait for a moment so he could return to his car and check his database. Reviewing my records wouldn't help him much. I had never been arrested on heist or assault charges in my youth. Just smoking weed, but it wouldn't appear.

I watched the deputy in my side mirror and saw him hang up his radio on his Jeep's dashboard. Then, he started walking with a notebook and a pen in his hand. I was now sure I'd have to give some money to the law enforcement officer. I sighed, slapping myself on the forehead as the officer came back to my car.

"Listen, officer," I began. "I've never got a ticket in my life. You can check, right?"

"I did," he said softly.

He smirked, but I didn't care. The man couldn't be much older than me. With his perfectly shaved chin and crewcut black hair, he was the spitting image of a rightful and faultless representative of the law.

"And?" I prodded. n

"I don't see why you should get away with it. The law is the law. If you break it, you need to take responsibility. Period."

OK. It was time to switch to Plan B.

I tried my secret weapon, even though it was questionable. But there were always tough choices in life. I didn't want to waste a hundred and fifty bucks on a stupid mistake. I tried batting my eyelashes, but his face remained impassive. Either the deputy was gay, or I was the worst actress on the planet.

"I am sorry," I finally declared.

Looked like I was going to be shelling out court costs. It was the sound of an engine. In fact, I could hear more than one. That was when I saw them.

Coming toward us was a big black van surrounded by three motorcycles like my father's. Shit, they would catch me red-handed. I probably looked stupid parked like that on the side of the road. I was hoping they would drive by without noticing me. But I had no such luck. They slowed down. One of the motorbikes, riding behind the van, overtook it. Its owner signaled them to keep on driving. The biker leading the convoy drove away. They were driving so slowly that I could see the guy in the passenger seat of the van nodding his head. He had short hair and a square jaw. He was a complete stranger to me.

Gale?

Then, the other two men slowed down and parked their motorcycles behind my car and the deputy's. I couldn't believe my eyes! I was probably flushed. The officer opened his eyes wide and looked at me quizzically. I shrugged innocently, clueless about what was going to happen. Letting go of my car door, he extended his arm to reach for his holster. With his other hand, he signaled the two men, who were walking to us, to stay away. I recognized Ash, who was approaching the deputy with a big smile on his face. He put his hands in the air to show he was harmless.

"Hi, Evan."

"Trevor," the deputy said dryly.

Trevor? Was it his real name? It was so unlike Ash. I was expecting something like Ashley, Ashton. But more importantly, I realized they knew each other well. An outlaw and a cop. Surprising. Monty Valley was a small town. Cohabitation between the club and the sheriff's office must have been complicated at times.

Ash walked to me and winked. I didn't know him enough to figure out if I could consider him an ally or if he was the enemy. He seemed close to my father, so he was probably there to help me. Behind him, I saw another member of the club I had never seen before. Was *he* Gale? Unlike his friend, he was rather tall and thin. There were no pumped-up muscles under the leather jacket. He looked young with his beardless face — way too young to have spent time in jail. He was looking at me with curiosity, but he avoided getting involved in the discussion between the two older guys.

"What the fuck are you doing here?" said the deputy.

"As you can see, just going for a drive. I just thought this young lady was in trouble."

His casual attitude made me smile. The guy had some nerve! He was making fun of an officer without blinking an eye. The deputy, Evan, gave me a quizzical look, then he turned his attention back to Ash.

"In fact, the young lady was driving too fast," Evan said. "Do you know each other?"

"You can say that," muttered the big dark-haired guy. "She's one of us."

I swallowed hard. Sooner or later, these guys would have to get their act together. The previous day, my father told the Sheriff that I was a customer. If I stayed around here, questions would be asked.

"I don't care!" Evan straightened. "The young lady was driving well over the speed limit. The law is the law, Trevor."

"It was a careless mistake!" I intervened, trying to defend myself.

Smiling, Ash pointed his finger at me. "You see? A careless mistake. Come on, Evan, let her go. She didn't kill anyone. On the other hand, the driver of the BMW, parked at exit 38, seems to be a big fish ..."

The cop twitched, and I saw a glimmer of hope.

"You're a pain in the ass, Trevor," Evan said wryly.

"I'm just trying to help!" Ash joked casually.

The deputy clenched his fists and his jaws. Then he turned to me, and I could read in his eyes that he was frustrated.

"I'll turn a blind eye on this one. Drive safely from now on. I never make the same mistake twice. Do the same."

He gave me my papers back, and I didn't need to be told twice to put them away. Still bewildered, I kept my mouth shut.

"Exit 38?" he asked Ash.

"Exit 38."

The deputy left, looking irritated and impatient.

"Say hi to Lizbeth!" Ash shouted over his shoulder.

Evan answered by giving him the finger. A few seconds later, the engine of his Jeep was roaring, and he disappeared over the horizon to chase more exciting prey. I couldn't believe my luck. I looked Ash up and down, not quite understanding how he had played this one out.

"What was that about?" I asked.

Shrugging, he said, "That was the sheriff's deputy, Evan Connor."

I still didn't know who the man was. Maybe he was making fun of me.

"Your father is waiting for us. We need to go," he added.

"Her father?" the second biker asked.

I looked at him for a moment and turned to Ash to get an explanation.

"Oh!" Ash said knowingly. "Joe, let me introduce you to... your brother, Casey. Jerry and Mona's son."

I almost choked. My... brother. He took a step towards me, and I felt his eyes scrutinizing every part of my face.

"Hi," he whispered.

"Hi," I answered foolishly.

A long silence followed. We looked at each other like two idiots. We were happy, I think. We were experiencing a life-changing moment.

"Come on, you guys. Your father is waiting for us. We need to go. You'll get to know each other when we arrive..."

I knew nothing about Ash, at least not until a week ago. Now, I knew a little bit more about the grumpy fifty-year-old man. He was strong-headed, proud, and smart. But he had interrupted a crucial moment in my life because we were late, and I resented it. Apparently, special occasions were not his strong point. On the other hand, he had voluntarily come to my rescue, even though he had just met me. It was a good point, and I was grateful.

"Let's go," I finally declared.

I hadn't planned to return to the complex this early, but it wasn't necessarily a bad thing. Everyone seemed to have converged there to welcome the famous Gale, so it would probably be a good idea to open the bar and help them celebrate. I turned on my Comet's engine and drove ahead to make a U-turn on the straight line. I drove slowly to Monty Valley, and in my side mirror, I noticed two dark shadows resembling dedicated bodyguards who were catching up with me. It was a strange feeling. It was new but not unpleasant.

14

JOE

It was the end of the afternoon when I walked through the Devil's Trip's door. It was too early to throw a party, but the buzzing activity within the room told me they were working on it. I found Mona with a box in her hands, and I greeted her. Realizing she had just received a delivery, I hurried to give her a hand and took another box that was lying on the hallway floor. I followed her into the back room, just behind the counter.

"Gale got out of jail," she explained. "We're going to celebrate tonight."

"I know. Jerry told me about it. I didn't know about the party, though. Are you going to need me?"

"You, but not only you! I also hired a few girls from the club. Alyson, Jenna, and Carole are coming to give us a hand."

"Other regulars?"

115

"No, they are sweeties. Gale is quite popular around here. We expect many people to celebrate his early release."

I made a quick mental check. Last weekend, Mona and I managed to take care of a crowded bar by ourselves. How many customers would justify hiring five more waitresses? I feared the worst.

"I've met your son," I said abruptly.

Mona put down another box on the back-room shelves and smiled as she wiped her hands to get rid of the dust.

"Oh? Did you see Casey?" she asked.

"Yes. He seems... very nice."

What could I say? I barely had the time to exchange two words with him.

"Yes, he's a good kid. He's walking in his father's footsteps. A real motorcycle addict."

In her voice, I heard unconditional love. In the meantime, Pacho walked into the bar, so I went back to the main room to greet him. He replied with a "Hi, Cutie," and I laughed. I was surprised to see him take his shift so early.

"With the party coming up," he said. "I need to think ahead."

How bad could it be? I let him go back to work and took care of putting the cans that had been delivered in the fridges. Then, someone knocked his fist against the counter, which startled me. As I stood up, my head hit the beer keg. I cursed, resenting my bad luck. Mona came back and smiled at the man who was responsible. Billy was laughing at me.

"Sorry, Gorgeous. I didn't think I would have this effect on you."

I grumbled but joined the odd grandpa. Billy must have been the oldest member of the club. He had thick gray and white hair and apple cheeks. He made me think of a Santa from hell. His broad shoulders were proudly wearing a Wild Crows' leather jacket. On its front pocket, a small embroidered piece of fabric mentioned he was the vice president of the club. Mona tenderly kissed him on the cheek, and I felt the deep connection that had been cementing their friendship during all those years.

The club was like a family. I realized it every time I witnessed the tight bond that was binding them. All the Wild Crows' members loved each other. The club was a fraternity aspiring to live by its own rules.

I heard the front door creak and an army of men wearing sunglasses walked in. There were three, to be exact. I immediately recognized Hanger with his almost bald head, his tattoos on his neck, and his dark skin. Just behind him was Casey. A spontaneous smile came to my lips. I didn't know him, but the simple fact that we shared the same father made me like him. His brown eyes were the focal point of his childish face. He looked like a kid dressed in his father's clothes. On his heels was the famous Gale, or so I thought. He was heavily built. He must have been in his forties. With his messy blond hair and his square jaw, I could have mistaken him for a respectable businessman or a family man. But the club's jacket told another story.

As soon as they walked through the door, Mona threw herself on his neck and embraced him. I was surprised to see how tight she was holding him. Under other circumstances, I would have found it strange. But I was starting to understand they were a family.

Casey walked to me with a shy smile. I leaned against the counter, probably to keep my composure, as I felt as uneasy as the first time we met.

"Hi again," he whispered.

"Hi again. So, we are..."

"Yeah, brother and sister," he said with a pout.

I nodded. There was no instruction manual to tell you how to behave in these situations. In fact, nobody knew what to do.

"It's great!" I said.

My tone was more enthusiastic than I thought it should be. I must have looked stupid, but my words came from the heart. My newfound brother laughed out loud as his hazel eyes were stuck on me.

"Yeah, it's great," he repeated.

"Show your face, old dog!"

Jerry's deep voice came from behind us. He was walking down the steps that led to the meeting room upstairs. With his legendary tact, my father walked to Gale. Mona stepped away. Then, they locked up in a manly embrace while their eyes expressed the depth of their friendship.

"Excuse me," said a feminine voice from the other side of the counter.

I turned my head around. A gorgeous young woman with black hair tied in a ponytail that went down below her elbow was talking to me. Her name was written on her metal necklace. Jenna. I immediately figured out who she was. She was one of the sweeties that would help out tonight. I smiled at her politely.

"Eh, excuse me, but what do you think you're doing?" she asked. "Are you new around here?"

I glanced at my younger brother, who was laughing in the corner of the room.

"Yeah, you could say that," I replied.

"She's my sister," Casey said with a mischievous wink.

The pretty brunette swallowed hard. Her eyes, locked on me, seemed apologetic. What was that about? *Good question.*

"Oh, Okay. I'm Jenna," she informed me.

"I know," I replied, pointing at her necklace.

She laughed and started working.

Casey turned his attention to me. "So, Sis, you are from Oregon, right?"

"You seem well informed."

"Mona is," he corrected me.

I should have thought of it. She was the matriarch in a group composed exclusively of men. She was respected by all, but she was also feared, so she brought some balance into this macho and manly world.

"How do you find it here?" Casey asked.

"It's okay. And if you consider that I am new to motor-bike clubs and nightclubs, I think I'm doing fine."

"That's what I've heard."

"Really? You seem to have heard a lot about me for someone who has just been back."

"It's not every day that your hidden sister turns up!"

He was right. Shayla, wearing a bag over her shoulder,

entered the Devil's Trip. I watched the clock. The party wouldn't start for another hour. I wondered if a stripper had to do warm-ups before a show, but I didn't ask. We greeted each other as soon as she finished hugging everyone.

Two more girls walked in. One was wearing Daisy Duke shorts, while the other one wore a very short dress. The heavy make-up gave away their identity. They were Carole and Alyson. The tall blond had an extravagant hairstyle, while her friend wore her brown hair in a soft bob. I immediately recognized the first one. She was the woman I saw wrapped around Mack's neck on my first shift at the bar. They gave me a quick "Hello."

My presence was not unanimously well accepted among the sweeties. The glances they gave me told the whole story. If they considered me as a threat, they were damn wrong. I wasn't there to steal one of their bikers. I had more ambition than to bed one of them with the hope of becoming "a regular." My ambition was to be part of a family, which was something I was missing. I wanted to find a new home where I could belong and feel safe.

Soon after, Mack and Ash walked through the Devil's door. The tall, dark-haired guy greeted those he hadn't seen before. Mack had a childish smile on his face. He was such a mischievous but touching child. His eyes were fixed on Gale. The two men got closer and scrutinized one another as they got face to face.

The ex-con spoke first. "You haven't changed! Still so fucking ugly!"

Mack stayed stone-faced, but his blue eyes were

sparkling. "And you're still a jackass, right? I've always known you were jealous of me, Bro!"

The entire room was silent. The second after, the two men hugged each other fiercely. They laughed and kept looking at each other.

"Damned, it has been so long!" Gale said happily.

I couldn't believe my eyes when I saw them head-butting each other. But I wasn't dreaming. The new guy put an arm around Mack's shoulders and waved his hand in the air.

"And I have every intention to make up for the last four fucking years!"

"Tonight is your night, Bro!" Billy shouted from the corner of the counter.

I immediately saw Ash walk to the jukebox, and I recognized the first notes of the song. Gale howled, making the crowd laugh. One of the men banged his fist against the counter to signal the party had started. Mona went behind the counter obediently.

Obviously, Gale would run the show tonight, even when it came to the time the party would start. I almost died laughing watching Casey standing on the pool table, acting like a rock star who played the guitar. Whistles rose in the room. Then, Bigma, Lazar, and Foxy joined us. It was only starting to get dark, but the party was already raging, and these men's livers were processing tons of alcohol.

Mack and Gale stuck together. It was a strange sensation not having him hovering over me. I almost felt disappointed. Many people had come to the Devil's to celebrate, and it was still early. Shayla had just finished the first part of her show. Her girlfriend, Noemy, a gorgeous blond with generous curves, was getting on stage. She made quite an impression on the crowd that was growing by the hour. When she was done, Ash decided he would be the DJ for the night, picking every song on the jukebox. When I went to parties, we just had regular sound systems. I wasn't even aware these machines still existed.

But that night, everything was different. Craziness was floating in the air. Eighties classics were a perfect match for the rock-n-roll atmosphere floating around. I served a round of beers to the members of the club sitting at the table, and I recognized the tall, dark-haired guy at the end of the counter. I brought him a drink and seized the opportunity to talk to him about what had happened earlier in the afternoon.

"Thanks for your help," I said to Ash. "I mean with the deputy."

"You're welcome."

He took a sip of his drink, then leaned over as if he wanted to confide in me. "I thought it would be better not to tell your father. He has better things to do right now."

"Good idea."

I saw a half-smile appear on his face.

"It was nice," I said. "You saved me from a costly fine."

"I like to help when I can."

Okay. Mr. Ash was a man of few words. Still, I tried to make him talk. After all, he was the only man not talking to someone else or hitting on a hot sweetie.

"Ash sounds nothing like Trevor."

His impenetrable blue eyes were fixed on me. It was unnerving. The color of his pupils was surreal. I had a hard time guessing his age. I could tell the story of his life had probably been going on for a few decades. Four or five, I would say. His many wrinkles showed life had been hard on him. His features weren't refined. They were sharp and raw. His cheeks were sunken, and his jaw was hidden by a beard as black as his hair. In short, Ash's face was noticeable.

"I guess not," he replied after a long pause.

If I wanted to know more about him, I would need to make him confess. What he didn't realize was that curiosity was one of my main flaws. It was in my genes.

"Where does your nickname come from?" I asked.

His eyes, sparkling dangerously, were still fixed on me. I wondered even more. I was as intrigued by him as he was by me.

"Try to guess."

"I don't know. Your middle name is Ashton?"

He laughed briefly before taking another sip. "Nope."

"Ashley? Ash..."

"Wrong again."

"Then, I give up."

"Already?" he said.

"I'm a poor loser."

Again, a dimple appeared on his cheek. "Ash, Ashes."

Smiling like an idiot, I slowly made sense of his half-spoken words. Then, my face turned white. "I am not sure I understand..."

"I think you do."

As in, he killed people and burned the bodies?

I was scared to death. His soft-spoken words frightened me. The blue color of his pupils was suddenly unnerving. All I could see in them was a silent threat. It was funny how fear could change how things looked in a heartbeat.

"Hey, Ash, look what I've found!"

Gale's voice jolted me, breaking the silent exchange between my eyes and Ash's. Still, I was somewhat relieved. The tall blond guy had just arrived with two pretty girls on his arm.

"Paulette and Georgia are bored, Bro!"

He gave him a big slap on the back, which made the tall, dark-haired man smile. I decided it was time for me to let them mind their own business while I would take care of mine. But a determined old wolf I had forgotten about resurfaced. A wolf named Mack. Mackenzie was his real name. I had guessed so from the conversations I had overheard. With a killer smile on his blond beard, trimmed into a long goatee, he shot me one of his meaningful glances.

"Jerry Junior," he teased me, "what do you say about hanging with me for a while? I enjoy your company."

He gave me a perfect smile, and for a split second, I was destabilized.

"Sorry, but I'm working," I answered with a wink.

He took my refusal with humor and pouted theatrically, which made me laugh. The next second, he was taking the lovely Shayla in his arms as a consolation prize. I laughed when I realized I had not been mistaken about him.

15

JOE

In my imagination, things should have gone like this. I should have attended to the customers until closing time, lost in the warm but unsettling atmosphere of the general drunkenness. Then, I would have gone home to my bed to enjoy a restful night. That was how I had envisioned the night. A vision in which everything would have gone down quietly. But they didn't know me. They didn't know my natural tendency to put myself in crazy situations.

It happened when Mona announced it was closing time. It was time for the last customers to say goodbye to the sweeties and their expert suggestive hip sways, but nothing went as planned. It would have been too simple. While people left the bar, the club's members remained inside. Jerry rolled down the iron shutter, blocking the access to the main door.

I immediately understood that the private party was about to start. No secret password was required to hang around, but you needed a leather jacket bearing a crow and a compass pointing west. The only exceptions were the sweeties like Jenna, Carole, Alyson, Mona, and Rebecca, who was Billy's regular.

My stepmom tapped me on the shoulder. "From now on, you relax, Sweetheart. It's an open bar."

I was baffled.

"No worries. Everything is under control."

"Oh."

That's all I could say. The carnage was about to start. Suddenly, I felt an arm around my shoulders, trying to pull me towards the open space. I jumped and saw Casey's inebriated smile.

"Come here, Sis!"

We sat on stools, and he handed me a beer. I thanked him as I grabbed it. After those crazy past hours, I gladly accepted the treat. The coolness of the glass felt good against my hands, which were covered in sweat. If I hadn't thought about cleaning up this mess the next morning, I would have enjoyed my drink more. My brother's hazel eyes were glassy, and his crooked smile made me laugh.

"So, tell me. What do you think of our little party?" he asked.

I joked as I tried to express my real feelings. "From the other side of the bar, it looks different."

He probably understood my point because he laughed out loud. "True, but you've settled in now!"

"You can say that," I said.

We cheered, and the beer tasted crisp and delicious. We talked about anything and everything. Even as drunk as he was, my brother wanted to change the world, and he chose me to implement his plan. I took the opportunity to get to know him better. It was easy to make a drunk man talk.

A sober woman would have an advantage. This was the perfect occasion, and he seemed inclined to talk about the members of the club. I looked at Mona and Jerry sweetly dancing to a slow tune, which Ash probably played for them on the jukebox. They were beautiful together. For a moment, I envied them. I enjoyed witnessing so much love between two people. Casey answered all my questions, and I got more answers in an hour than during the last few days. In return, I had to give in to his demands. For each answer I got, I had to take a sip of alcohol. I was soon engaged in a stupid and immature game, but it worked perfectly. Miss Detective soon became Miss Laughing Out Loud. I had so many questions to ask.

He told me that Foxy's real name was Adam and that his nickname came from his red locks. Bigma's name was Marcus. He was a tall and strong man, which was how they had come up with that name. Lazar came from Lazarus, and I was surprised to learn that this name still existed. It sounded so old-fashioned! Mack was short for Mackenzie and Gale for Gaylord. A name from another time. It was amazing. Then I asked him about his name and Jerry's. My dad had no nickname. They just called him "the boss." Casey hadn't proved himself yet, at least not enough to earn this badge of honor. Time would take care of it. He was still very young. I was surprised to learn he was eager to get one, as it would be solid proof he belonged to the club. I suddenly realized that we had omitted to talk about two members.

"How about Hanger?" I asked.

The number of beers I drank undoubtedly gave me courage. Casey's lips winced.

"It's just Hanger," he replied.

He was lying. I could smell it. Deep inside of me, I knew that I should control my curiosity. So far, Casey had been honest with me, so it would be a mistake to get on the wrong side of him.

"And Ash? He told me that his nickname came from ashes."

Casey drank his beer straight before pouring himself another one. I noticed that the proximity of the keg was probably not a coincidence.

"Yeah, that's right," he said.

"I still don't understand."

"What don't you understand?"

He was looking at me as if I were the stupidest person on earth, and I blushed. All the beer I had drunk was starting to affect my capacity to think straight.

"The ashes!" I told him, rolling my eyes.

I was sure those were his words, and I went straight to the point before I would lose focus.

"Is he an arsonist?" I insisted, throwing my hands in the air.

I glared at him. I could take nothing for granted with these men. My brother laughed out loud.

"Not quite. His style is more... explosive."

He was whispering to my ear, leaning closer to me. Why was he doing that? It was common knowledge around here. They all knew each other. I was flabbergasted. Explosives? What would he need them for?

"You're talking about fireworks or things like that, right?"

Puzzled, I looked at him. The truth and its violence frightened me. I wanted to hear it, but on the other hand, not knowing was comforting. I knew my question sounded hollow, and I probably sounded stupid and naïve. But I had to ask, which would leave no other choice than to hear the answer.

"Not exactly, no."

I tried to analyze Casey's smile. He wasn't lying. This time, I served the next round of beers. I drank mine straight. It helped me process the information, or so I thought. Was Ash making bombs explode? I was so afraid to speak these words out loud that I put my hand over my mouth. His eyes were half-closed, and my brother laughed at me. At that point, I was ready to hear everything, or almost.

"It leaves us with Hanger. You lied through your teeth. Even if I am drunk, I know it. What's the problem? Why don't you tell me everything?"

My brother looked at me seriously.

"Hanger," he said, mimicking a hangman.

My tired brain slowly processed each sound that came

through his mouth. Then, I did it repeatedly. Had I heard it right? Hanger...

"What the fuck?"

I needed some water, not beer.

Casey seemed to read my mind, but we continued to drink the golden nectar. Reflecting on the information I got, I tried to put things into perspective. When Ash had talked about himself earlier in the evening, I had jumped to the worst conclusion. I had seriously considered he could be a murderer. He had tricked me, the bastard. He took advantage of my ignorance and probably got a good laugh out of it. Still, I was relieved he wasn't a killer. From what I had heard, he was just blowing up... what was it again? Buildings. Empty buildings. But how could I be sure they were empty? Good Lord...

I hoped so. I felt like I was an amateur actress in a detective series. And Hanger, the man, was so cold... I looked at him sitting with Billy at the other end of the room. I shivered. I knew he had killed before. I had stepped into a strange world. Unwillingly, I had entered a world of corruption and deception I couldn't have imagined. All I wanted was to meet my father. The bikers with their leather jackets had frightened me in the beginning, but not anymore. Damned! Besides motorcycles, I was being introduced to trafficking, ex-cons, weapons, explosives, ...and murderers?

I kind of knew the club wasn't legit. I was not born yesterday. But this? For god's sake, this was... too much. Too much at once. My heart was beating like crazy in my chest. I thought of the bombs. Was Ash planting them? Fuck!

I couldn't care less about being polite! Another beer helped me settle my nerves, and Casey was laughing as he read my face. The music and the Devil's atmosphere made me even more nervous. The tall, dark-haired man leaning nonchalantly on the jukebox gave me a bloodcurdling look. The woman called Georgia–or it might have been her friend, Paulette–was giving him a lap dance.

She must have been in her twenties. Her make-up had smeared, probably because of the heat. He smiled at me, which was totally inappropriate. Was he now laughing because he had managed to scare me to death? Did he know his trick had worked? While his fearless sweetie, Georgia or Paulette, was executing a series of suggestive movements that his drunken mind couldn't misinterpret, Ash finished his drink and cheered while he was still observing me. I found it disgusting.

"Why would you do that?" I asked.

I stopped talking as I realized that Casey had just fallen asleep on the wooden counter. Great! Not only was I completely drunk, but there was no one around to talk with. It was time to sneak out. I would clean up tomorrow. Nobody would notice if I was there or not. I got up from my stool clumsily and staggered to the coat hanger. As I grabbed my jacket, I was shocked to discover Foxy shamelessly groping Carole in a dark corner next to me, and I gasped. Things were becoming ugly around here. I noticed that none of them seemed to be considering seeking privacy. Having an audience didn't bother them. He lifted her skirt while I froze in front of such indecent behavior.

I finally turned around to see how bad things were in the bar–and also to avoid witnessing the hot scene that was unfolding before my eyes. Others were trying to do the same in dark corners or in plain sight.

Mona and Jerry had run off without telling anyone. They had taken the back door, of course, as the main entrance was locked. It was so clever of them, and I had every intention of doing the same. Suddenly, a hand grabbed my wrist, and before I could understand what was happening, I found myself pressed against somebody. Shit!

Mack's killer smile made me feel uneasy. The bad boy's blue-gray eyes and his blond hair reminded me that wolves were prowling at night. And there was more than one tonight. This one didn't let go easily. The way he was looking at me touched my heart, but the feeling didn't last. I quickly remembered why I couldn't give in to him. The bastard! I was sure he was conscious of the effect he had on women. And he would be right. He was Machiavellian, vicious, but so sexy. I pushed him away with the back of my hand.

"I am not interested, Mack. But thanks."

Despite my efforts to sound convincing, my smile showed my true feelings. Alcohol had an unfortunate tendency to make me weak. But I had to be strong. My words didn't seem to discourage him, though. That man liked a challenge. It was something I needed to remember, but it was not surprising. This type of guy thrived on confrontations. It made the chase more exciting, and I was his new prey. He would get over it, or so I hoped. His smile widened, and he held me closer. My heart raced. He was whispering in my ear. I shivered.

"No? For sure? Your loss."

Humility was not his strong point! I was expecting

him to let go of me, but I suddenly felt his warm lips over mine. The blond beard covering his square jaw scratched my cheeks, but I didn't push him away, and I let myself go. Despite my will, my body reacted to his touch. I felt like I was losing my senses. The unexpected kiss soon became more confident and deliberate. I let him kiss me, enjoying feeling his large hands wandering on my lower back.

"Hey, Mack!"

Moving away from me, he grumbled. I was stunned. With a broad smile on her face, a pretty girl with short hair interrupted my special moment with Mack. I stepped aside, embarrassed by this moment of weakness.

"Shelby," he said seductively. I didn't move when he took us both by the arm. "Girls, how about you and I go to a more private place?"

I didn't know if I was more surprised or outraged, maybe both. My mouth formed an "O," but no sound came out. In the meantime, his new girlfriend had agreed, and I froze. Anger rose throughout my body. I was mad at myself. What an idiot! His pickup line was straightforward, and I should have understood immediately. Instead, I got carried away for a few seconds, and there I was, looking like an idiot. I pushed away his arm and turned, giving him a stink eye.

"I told you, Mack. I'm not interested. Have a good night!"

I faked a smile and clicked my heels before walking towards the back door. I walked through the room, ignoring everyone in my path. Casey was still at the counter, in Morpheus's arms. I was about to get out through the back door when the jukebox tricked me. No. It was actually Ash who was responsible for playing the tune *Riders on the Storm* by the Doors. I was annoyed. Was he trying to mess with me?

I turned around, already angered by the predictable behavior of the club's Don Juan. Still leaning against the machine, the fifty-year-old man, addicted to explosives, was laughing while he was observing my reaction. His drunken black-haired girlfriend was still performing her provocative dance, but he didn't seem interested.

At that moment, my fear of him was enough to entertain him. I grumbled and decided I would settle the score before I left. I was new around here, that was true. I was also completely drunk, but I wasn't prepared to become the new toy everybody could play with. I considered myself open-minded, especially given everything I had seen since my arrival. I accepted the rules without asking a lot of questions.

That's what I was expected to do, and I tried my best to accept them unconditionally. In return, I deserved some respect. It had to go both ways, or it wouldn't work. I wasn't a sweetie looking for a husband. I was the boss's daughter, and if I didn't set the limits on how they could behave around me, things could turn nasty. I had to treat them like kids. Bad, beaten, and uncontrollable kids who had access to explosives and weapons, too... What the hell!

I walked confidently to the tall, dark-haired man, not paying any attention to the close-eyed woman, who was in a trance. The Doors were singing about a killer on the loose, and Ash seemed to find it funny. His eyes were fixed on me. They were blue, so incredibly blue. He made me really nervous. The pretty brunette looked at me. Then she glanced briefly at the biker before her quizzical, half-closed eyes went back to me.

"Go on. Don't mind me," I protested. "I don't care. I just want to say two words to your friend."

The angrier I got, the more entertained the tall guy in front of me seemed to be. What could be more annoying?

"You really screwed with me earlier, Ash." I voluntarily deepened my voice as I pronounced his nickname. "Ashes, right? Now, I know. And it wasn't funny." I continued.

He looked at me for a moment before laughing out loud. "To tell you the truth, it was pretty funny. You should have seen your face!"

His designated dancer had already forgotten about me, and she resumed her provocative movements against his body. Damn! Modesty was not part of their DNA.

"I guess it's a kind of hazing," I said. "But now, it's over. The newbie is going to show you what she's made of!"

His lips formed a fine line. "I can't wait."

"Fine."

They were wrong about me, and I needed to show them. Intoxicated, I climbed on the pool table and whistled to get the attention of all the bikers in the room.

"I want things to be clear! I am new around here, but I ain't stupid, guys!" I said with my finger circling on top of my head to illustrate my words. "I might be the boss's daughter, but I am also Joe. I'm a nice girl as long as you respect me. It goes both ways. So, if you want things to go smoothly, start to take me seriously, got it?"

Without a word, I climbed down. I heard a few laughs,

and someone was applauding while others whistled. I didn't care and left. Luckily, my apartment was just around the corner. Even though I only had three flights of stairs to climb, it took me two attempts to finally reach my door. As I was trying to get home, my stomach protested. Or was it my liver? When I finally made it, I threw myself onto the bed, fully clothed.

16

JOE

A warm shower the next morning. It was my only relief... so to speak. Being drunk was not part of my routine. At least not for the last few years. Ten years ago, it was another story. Recently, though, I lived a more responsible and stable life. The terrible headache that was raging through my skull reminded me I had made the right choice to quit. The hot water running on my skin felt like my only chance to cure my hangover. I had drunk too much, no doubt about that, and the memories that were rushing back to my mind were not pleasant ones.

I couldn't say I had been smart. Not only had I let a notorious womanizer kiss me, but I had to make a fool of myself in front of an assembly of drunken bikers, among which there were a killer and an arsonist. He and his damned explosives. I put a hand on my forehead, trying to erase all the memories of last night from my sore brain. It didn't work. I remembered every piece of information given by my brother, who had been even more intoxicated than me. Maybe I would have preferred to forget some parts of his confession, like the one about Hanger, the executioner, and Ash, the bomb expert...

When I came to Monty Valley, my only goal was to meet my father. Fate had decided to make it harder on me, as he was involved in arms trafficking. It was surreal. My life seemed to be a remake of *The Godfather*. M. Coppola would have been impressed. Had my father told me everything? I wasn't convinced, given what Casey had shared with me. Poor guy! I had used sneaky tactics to make him talk. Finally, I turned the water off, thinking that it was useless to obsess over this. It wouldn't solve anything or give me the answers I was looking for.

I draped a towel around me and went to the living room with my eyes half-closed to avoid the morning light. I'd have loved to sleep until the afternoon, but I remembered I had left the Devil's Trip without cleaning up. I didn't want to think about it...

What could have happened after I had gone? I started to feel sick to my stomach, just trying to imagine it. Or maybe it was the large amount of beer I had drunk all night. I went into the kitchen with only one thing on my mind, and it was the coffee machine. Half awake, I stumbled on things I thought were clothes thrown on the floor last night. Reaching the third floor safely had been quite an accomplishment, and I was in no state to keep things tidy. I jumped when I heard the mass of clothes grumble.

"What the fuck are you doing here?" a voice grumbled.

I couldn't believe my eyes! Mackenzie was curled up on my sofa. His legs were stretched out in front of him. He grumbled and turned around to avoid seeing my anger. I wouldn't let him get away with it this time.

"Hey!" I shouted, kicking his shoes.

I got his attention.

"Easy!" he complained, raising his hands over his head.

"Get up and get out!" I declared with my arms crossed over my chest.

When he clumsily stood up, I heard his knee pop. Apparently, I wasn't the only one who had too much last night. He winced, but I detected a sparkle of amusement in his blue eyes. I got angrier.

"Easy," he said. "I just slept on your sofa. Don't get yourself all worked up..."

"How did you get in?"

"It was open. You must have forgotten to lock your door."

"Do you break into people's homes when they forget to lock the door?" I scolded him.

"Just yours."

Okay. He was playing games with me. Why wasn't I surprised? I grabbed him by the t-shirt and dragged him to the door.

"Out!" I said, pointing to the door.

Once again, he raised his hands in the air and made a sorry face that was almost convincing. "I came to apologize. I behaved like an asshole. The door was unlocked, and you were not answering, so I walked in. You were already sleeping. You were drunk as a skunk."

"Such a nice thing to say."

He laughed and continued explaining. "That's when I saw the sofa... It was either this or a booth at the bar. I wouldn't have been able to drive my bike. So..."

"So you chose my sofa," I interrupted him.

"Bingo!"

I looked at him for a moment. He seemed sincere, but I didn't trust this guy. He knew how to manipulate people, and he had proved it to me last night. In my defense, I had let down my guard because I was drunk. Otherwise, I wouldn't have given in so easily.

"You're right," I said. "You behaved like an asshole."

Again, he was amused by my anger. It drove me crazy.

"I simply suggested a group activity," he said mischievously. "I had to try..."

I sighed. He was so childish. A forty-year-old child full of charm and sex appeal. But he was also full of vice and depravity.

"I am not the kind of girl that lies on her back like that, Mack. Do you get it?"

"I don't see what you're talking about."

"Hell yeah, you do," I said, pushing my finger in his chest. "That's what sweeties want, but not me. It must be exciting having groupies ready to fulfill all your needs! But you forget there's the real world out there. We call it a normal life. That's where I come from. And I don't need your approval to be here. I'm Jerry's daughter. I don't intend to be your next trophy or anyone else's. You were lucky my father didn't witness your little game last night."

He winced. I had finally managed to erase his irritating smile from his face. "I probably wouldn't be here to talk about it. Or I would be missing an arm or a leg ..."

I was petrified, not knowing if he was serious or not, but I kept my calm. Frowning with my arms crossed, I looked at him, totally oblivious of my outfit. The towel wrapped around me revealed parts of my naked body. It was like trying to offer water to an alcoholic in a bar full of whiskey. He must have noticed I was embarrassed, as he laughed out loud before passing me to go into the kitchen.

"Nice PJs."

Okay. He had noticed. Without asking me, he poured two cups of coffee and gave me one. I surrendered and accepted it while mumbling to myself. I sat on a stool, and he stood right in front of me. I took a sip, which helped me relax for a second.

"Make yourself at home," I said.

He answered with a crooked smile. Then, he drank his coffee silently. His eyes were still fixed on me. I think I blushed once or twice, or was it the whole time? I realized I had to change clothes. I had enough of his eyes wandering over me, and I needed some privacy. I couldn't risk it.

"You didn't say no," he observed casually.

I almost choked on my coffee.

"I was completely drunk," I said defensively.

"I've always been told that it wasn't an excuse."

"For me, it's different. I don't drink."

His eyes searched my face for a moment. "So, are you saying that you let anyone kiss you when you are drunk?"

His raised eyebrow gave away the hidden meaning of his words. At that moment, I hated him more than ever.

"No, but shit happens."

"I see."

A broad smile spread across his face. While he was finishing his coffee, I observed his strange hairstyle. His hair was shaven on the sides, and he kept the top long enough he could braid it or occasionally tie his hair in a ponytail.

"And when I put my hands on your waist to pull you closer, you didn't protest. You even encouraged me."

"Bullshit!"

"The way you kissed me did."

"Whatever! You won't let me have the last word." I pointed my finger at him as a warning. "One thing is for sure, though. My ass won't end up between your sheets, Mack."

I thought I had made myself clear, but apparently, Mack didn't agree. I heard the metallic sound of his belt as he was undoing it, and his jeans dropped to the floor. The next moment, he had taken off his T-shirt, revealing a pale chest covered with fine blond hair. From his shoulders down, his body's fine muscles were exposed. For a few seconds, I couldn't think straight. When I came back to reality, I was shocked.

"What are you doing?"

My outraged expression seemed to arouse him.

"I stink of alcohol," he complained, just wearing his black boxers over his private parts. "You said your ass wouldn't end up in my bed. What about the shower?"

He gave me a broad smile, showing all his teeth. He

seemed satisfied with himself. His arrogance was unnerving. Walking like a tiger, he went into the bathroom as if he owned the place. The guy had nerve. When I saw a piece of black fabric land in the corridor, I sighed. Then, I heard the water being turned on.

While he was showering, I changed into more appropriate clothes and tied my hair while I was thinking about how I would throw him out. I couldn't bear his sense of entitlement anymore. Provocation and hitting on women were second nature to him. When he returned about ten minutes later, the scent of my body soap filled the room. It was nicer to smell exotic flowers than alcohol, which was making me nauseous. He was handsome as a god and proud as a peacock as he came into the room with only my towel wrapped around his waist.

"I guess your ass didn't want to join me under the shower," he said.

"How smart of you!" I said with a wince.

Then, I put the mugs in the sink, not minding him, as he dressed as slowly as he could. I only raised my eyes when he walked to me, fully dressed in his t-shirt, his jeans, and his jacket.

"Now get out!" I ordered.

"Already?"

I frowned.

"Okay, easy!" he protested, putting his hands over his head.

I walked him to the door with every intention of locking it after him. One uninvited guest was enough in one day! But the blond devil, standing in front of me, had other plans. He turned around, his eyes teasing me.

"Wait, I was thinking..."

"What?"

His presence drove me nuts.

"You and I get along..." he said.

He was apparently waiting for an answer. I looked at him and laughed. "You are kidding, right?"

"Really, I'm serious. I enjoy teasing you, and you like to threaten me. We are becoming good friends."

"If you think so... Then what?"

"I'm attracted to you, and like it or not, you like me. You proved it yesterday. Even if you were drunk," he continued before I could say a word.

I sighed.

"What about being sex friends?" he asked innocently.

I chocked.

"Get out!"

I opened the door wide, not caring about him being seen leaving my apartment. I would find an excuse. I had nothing to be ashamed of.

He hesitated. "Hey, maybe your father is out there..."

"You are old enough to take care of yourself, no?" I said, the irony not lost on either of us. "The worst that could happen is him taking care of your private parts. Believe me, it would be a good thing for all women out there."

A shocked expression came across his face. I exulted.

"Go away! Get out, Mack!"

I pushed him brutally and slammed the door in his face.

After he left, I sighed. The guy was incredibly intrusive.

17

JERRY

The last days had been rough. Gale had returned to his routine. He had earned the right to wear this leather jacket again after four years of detention, during which he had never betrayed the club. He had been arrested for drug dealing, and it was the main reason we stopped trafficking. Even though it was lucrative. But the feds were after us, and they were watching our every move. Gale was caught while he was transporting several kilos of drugs for the San Francisco Black Wolves.

Even though the name of the club was always hanging in the air during his interrogation, Gale refused to open his mouth. Yet, a deal with the officer in charge of the investigation, a man named Hornett, had saved him from the ten years usually intended for this crime. In exchange for information about a rival gang, his sentence was reduced. He had been encouraged to take the deal, even though retaliation was highly probable.

The Kasabov were our sworn enemies. And it wasn't likely to change, as we planned to control arms trafficking in the Reno area. Sometimes, our line of business meant working hand in hand with our rivals, but not them. And this had been an excellent opportunity to weaken them so we could take over their territory. Therefore, Gale had spilled the beans. His sentence was reduced to five years because of his loose tongue. He'd gotten out in four because of good behavior.

I went to the workshop early in the morning. A customer had entrusted a magnificent 1965 Chevrolet Impala SS to me. It was like an early Christmas present for the guys.

Working on such a gem was like caring for a newborn for these men addicted to mechanics. When I arrived, I greeted Ash, who was leaning over the engine. Billy came a few minutes later, wearing a t-shirt covered in oil. I couldn't help laughing. The younger ones were not up yet. I should have known. It was something to get used to. Unless there was an emergency, they were not early risers. At noon, the cherry red rocket with chrome accents would be surrounded by a crowd. The customer wanted to be sure it was in good condition. It was a legacy. I quickly checked the vehicle, and I was speechless. It was gorgeous, a real gem. I usually preferred motorcycles, but this kind of collectible could have made me change my mind in a heartbeat.

"I can't believe the owner doesn't give a damn about it," Ash whispered in a disgusted tone.

"He wants to auction it," Billy explained.

I smiled. Money was the sinews of war.

"Such a waste," I added.

My phone vibrated in my pocket, and I took the call. It came from an unknown number.

"This is Welsh," I answered.

"Hi, Jerry."

I froze. At the other end of the line, I heard a broken voice, speaking with a strong accent... I immediately recognized it. It was Suerte Ramirez's.

"Suerte," I greeted him.

That damned Mexican got his nickname after surviving an incredible number of life-threatening events. He was a walking miracle, according to my men. I distanced the phone from my ear, fully aware that this call was a priority. We were not friends or even allies. Hanger and Bigma's performance might also have threatened our future collaboration. It had been a total fiasco because of the Russians.

"How is business going these days, Jerry?"

I was perfectly aware he hadn't called to have a casual talk. His proper introduction was unnerving.

"What do you want, Suerte? You're not calling me to talk about the workshop and the bar, are you?"

I heard him laugh, which made me believe I wasn't mistaken.

"You're right. Politeness suits you though," he joked. "I want us to meet to go over this little deal of yours."

There was a hushed silence.

"My men told you about the deal when you met," I inferred.

"Yeah, they did. And they did more than that. Next time, send me some men who don't have a temper. We don't need to attract attention."

I grumbled. I was aware that my guys had messed up. "How could we guess that the crew would join the party?"

"I didn't know either. But your guys fired first. If we do business together, I don't want it to happen again. Keep your dogs on a leash, Jerry."

At that moment, I wished I could have shot him just because he had insulted my brothers. But doing business required self-control, and it was easier to be hundreds of miles away from him.

"It won't happen again."

I hated to knuckle under to anyone, but it was sometimes necessary to do business.

"Okay," said Suerte. "Let's meet at the warehouse, a few miles after exit 279 towards Carlin. I'll be there at 3.00 p.m. Don't be late."

I agreed. "I'll be there."

I hung up immediately, my eyes fixed on the horizon. I didn't trust Suerte. He was unstable and acted depending on his personal interests. But who didn't in our line of business? Dog eat dog. Today's enemies would probably become tomorrow's allies. When money was in the balance, all was fair. The winner took it all. Often, it was the smartest one. Betrayals and screw-ups were part of the routine.

Loyalty was reserved for the members of your own club. I went back to my guys. We needed to be prepared. It was critical for us to outsmart the Russian's brutes. Despite Suerte's relatively friendly tone, each meeting with the Bandoleros was risky. Nothing could be taken for granted. Things could change quickly and without notice.

It was a three-hour drive to the meeting point. As expected, the warehouse was the ideal place to shoot someone without being heard or seen. The gloomy atmosphere was a perfect reminder to be on my guard. Lost in the middle of nowhere, at the end of a dirt road that separated two deserted valleys, I saw the sheet metal building that would serve as our meeting point. As we were driving by, I didn't spot any Russian guards, but I still kept my eyes open. During the last encounter, they didn't show up at the very beginning. They had to be there, hidden somewhere.

· · ·

As soon as we got off our bikes, I saw Suerte and two of his bodyguards walking toward us. They were coming out of the warehouse, and they stopped a few feet away, waiting for us to come forward. Instinctively, my hand stroked my holster. In case of a problem, I would be ready. It had become a habit of mine, and it was comforting. It was one of those superstitious rituals athletes do before a big competition. Ash and Billy were on my heels, and we cautiously walked towards Suerte. The Mexican extended his hand, and I vigorously shook it. He also greeted my men, who had their hands on their belts, as a sign things could eventually turn nasty.

"Follow me!"

When we walked through the door, we entered a dark space lit by a few neon lights. Roots were growing every-where in this abandoned place, and it smelled of dirt and dust, maybe of rust, too. Suerte invited us to sit around a small table that had been set up in the back of the room. He wasn't that tall, but his broad shoulders were intimidat-ing. He was also a loose cannon. We had been working separately for years, but all in all, we managed to stay on good terms.

Things were fine between us. He sat on a chair and invited us to do the same. I chose the one in the middle, and my guys sat around me. Standing further away, I noticed two heavily armed men wearing leather jackets with the Bandoleros' logo on them. The third one was hardly visible, hidden in the opening of an office door. If things went south, we would be outnumbered. I clenched my jaw and listened to Suerte.

"So, let's not beat around the bush," he said. "You have

weapons for me. But as you know, I already have a supplier. Why would I do business with you?"

His accent was getting on my nerves. I tried to ignore it. "I thought my men had already filled you on this..."

"Yeah, they did. But I want to hear it from you, Jerry. I'm not convinced..."

His satisfied smile made me cringe. I cleared my throat and tried to maintain my poker face, even though the Mexican was getting on my nerves. I mimicked him, joining my hands together on the table.

"I can deliver ten times more weapons than the Kasabovs. And twice as fast."

"You're more expensive," he observed.

"Not the same thing. We're not talking about low-quality firearms that feed the war in the Middle East. We're talking about high-end weapons that can't be traced. Do you know what that means, Suerte?"

He pouted, and I carried on with my experienced salesman's speech. "It means you won't find a better deal on the market. In Russia, people may rely on quantity, but here, it is all about quality. Try out our products, and you'll never go back to the shit manufactured in Russia. You might want to order some for resale, but for your crew, it's a no-brainer. My suppliers have their own series, but they also manufacture improved copies of all models available on the market with a better finish. The Irish don't play by the same rules, Suerte. Dealing with them lets us bypass the usual channels and dodge every U.S. database out there. No way to trace the purchase back to anyone on a watchlist. And on top of that, we've still got solid ties with the IRA. You know as well as I do—that kind of connection always pays off."

The leader of the Bandoleros was intently listening to me. I could feel he wasn't entirely convinced. It was time to put my last card on the table.

"And I didn't come empty-handed."

I typed a short text message on my cell phone while my customer stared at me. A minute later, I heard the deafening sound of a roaring engine, followed by a knock on the door. Suerte ordered one of his men to open it. Lazar was standing there with a rolling suitcase, looking like a gray-haired Goliath. He walked to us and threw it carelessly on the table. I winked at him, and he left right away. I had successfully achieved the first part of my plan.

Suerte gave me a quizzical look before opening my little present. Inside, he found several weapons, including a Glock 19, an M4 rifle, and a machine gun with a laser sight.

"It's just a sample. I've got way more than these three models. But I chose the best ones so you could get a taste of what I have in store."

I could feel I was scoring points. Suerte nodded his head, showing me he appreciated my present, and I had just proved to him I could pleasantly surprise him with an unexpected visit from one of my men. He grabbed the Glock and loaded it. He defiantly pointed it at me, but I didn't shift. He was smiling like a kid on Christmas morning. Unexpectedly, he turned towards the wall behind him and shot twice at a paper target I hadn't even noticed. I guessed he wanted to check the weapon's accuracy. He did the same with the other two firearms. The bullets of the machine gun left multiple holes in the metal sheet, but he didn't seem to care. We were far enough from any inhabited zone to be noticed by someone. When Suerte put the weapons back into their case, his eyes were still locked on them.

"I told you. A no-brainer," I continued confidently.

He nodded pensively. "I must admit it was fun!"

He gave us a broad smile that revealed all his teeth. At that moment, I understood I had won.

"You need to do something about the price, Jerry."

I sighed and thought about it for a moment. "If your order is big enough, I can lower the price."

Suerte stroked his chin, looking suddenly serious.

"You know the Kasabovs. They are no angels. They won't let you take their business away from them. I don't want to be caught in the middle of another war."

"Let me take care of this."

He seemed satisfied with my answer. "I don't want my men to be involved. Otherwise, we are done."

"You have my word. I'll take care of the Kasabovs myself."

"You don't know who you're dealing with," Suerte said.

I was about to answer when we heard several cars driving at high speed outside, followed by the sound of brakes. Suerte looked concerned. I smiled confidently, which made him even more confused.

"I know that. And I'm ready to get down to it right now!"

I jumped from my chair, followed by my men.

"How do you say 'Hello' in Russian?" Ash joked

Billy warned our new partner. "It's time to pick a side, old man!"

Suerte seemed to hesitate. Then he pulled out his gun and pointed it in front of him. With a simple jerk of the head, he ordered his men to do the same. Our little army was getting bigger. I moved first and kicked the sheet metal door open. Now, we were about to get to the next part of my plan. Russians were so predictable... Two black Jeeps were parked in front of us. A white van was waiting a little bit further down the road. I couldn't help but laugh when I spotted it.

Men jumped from the two Jeeps with machine guns pointed at us. They reacted exactly as I expected. I raised my hands in the air and tried to talk to them, especially to the tall, heavily built man standing in front of me. I had recognized the eldest of the Karamazov brothers, Sergei.

"Hey, calm down! We're just paying a visit to our old mate, Suerte."

As I spoke, I smiled broadly to annoy them.

"Are you fucking kidding me?" Sergei demanded.

After chatting with Mexicans, we were now about to get an earful from men with an Eastern accent. Just perfect!

"Get the truck and all the guns!" ordered the Russian big boss to his men.

"Fuck!" screamed Ash.

He stepped forward, and before I could stop that idiot, Sergei fired his gun. I heard a single shot followed by a sharp, shrill noise. The bastard! Ash had been shot and was now lying on the ground. The bullet had grazed his right thigh, and he was writhing in pain, blood pouring out of his wound. Luckily, it didn't seem life-threatening.

"Game over!" Sergei said. "My patience is wearing thin."

The big boss talked in Russian to one of his men, a thin guy with a shaved head covered in tattoos. He opened the doors of the white van, and three men who had followed him quickly unloaded the boxes that were inside. Sergei opened one of them while his crew was loading the others in the two black Jeeps. He pushed away the car parts that were used as decoys. He pulled out a Glock and roared like a beast as he exhibited it.

"Assholes! Did you think you would get away with it?"

While Sergei Karabasov was probably getting excited by the thought of burying us in a few minutes, I enjoyed anticipating what was coming. I was about to crush him as the insignificant insect he was. The man was so full of himself that he was totally blind. I think I even let out a smile. Behind us, Suerte and a dozen Bandoleros started to shoot straight in front of them. I jumped towards Ash and pulled him behind the line formed by the bikes of the Mexicans.

"You'll have to wait, Bro!" I informed him.

Writing on his side, he grumbled. I gave him my bandana so he could apply it to his wound. Then, Billy joined us, and we protected ourselves from the gunfire. A few Russians were killed on the spot, but they were not key men in the organization. Sergei's brother was nowhere to be seen, which was probably a safety measure. The two heads of the Kasabov empire couldn't risk their lives in the same location and at the same moment. It would be too risky if things went south.

The first Jeep drove away with screeching tires. Inside was the eldest of the Russian Mafiosos. We aimed at its passengers and started to shoot. The driver managed to escape the bullets, and he drove off right behind the first vehicle. Outside, only one guy had survived the attack. He quickly surrendered, throwing his weapon on the ground. Still surprised by the man's cowardice and credulity, I sighed. Billy walked to him and shot him in the head. Then, a deafening silence filled the warehouse, which was full of dust after the Jeeps had left hastily. Suerte looked at me quizzically, and he seemed annoyed.

"You should take care of this!"

"That's exactly what I'm doing," I replied calmly.

At that moment, we heard a loud bang coming from a few hundred feet away. Then flames and smoke rose through the air. A lot of smoke.

"See?" I stared at Suerte, who seemed satisfied. "Two boxes of unusable weapons and old rusted car parts—gone in flames."

I'd set the trap well. The Russians had driven off in rigged vehicles. Suerte seemed flabbergasted and finally nodded his head. I even saw a quirky smile appear on his face.

"We need to clean this up before the cops show up," he said.

I nodded. Lazar joined us with a satisfied look on his face. When he saw Ash lying on the ground, he helped him get on his feet.

"Come on, Bro! I need to drive you back. A three-hour

drive is not gonna be pleasant, but that gem of yours worked wonders. Just saying…"

I helped them. Ash was a former bomb disposal expert in the Marines. His expertise was priceless. We installed him on a blanket in the back of the van. I pulled out a bottle of whiskey from a box hidden in a corner and gave it to him.

"Have a safe trip, old mate!"

I slapped him gently on the shoulder, and he smiled at me despite the pain. He was a real tough guy. Maybe the toughest of us all. We closed the doors, and Lazar drove our wounded friend back to Monty Valley. I just had time to slip Joe's number in his hand so she would have time to find a first aid kit before meeting us at the Devil's. Going to a hospital was out of the question. It would be faster to surrender to the police. The van left, and I walked back to Suerte. He looked at me, probably wondering what he should do next.

"You know his brother is coming after us, now…"

"I know," I said. "I'll take care of it."

"In the same way that you just did? You were lucky we were here. Now, we are both screwed."

I looked at him, knowing he was right. "Yeah, I owe you one."

"Prove it when you send me the invoice. I want two hundred Glocks and a hundred M4s by next month."

I repressed a laugh. After the adrenaline rush, I was on edge. For the whole day, I had kept my doubts and my fears to myself, but I was just pretending. It was necessary for my line of business. Bluffing was sometimes the only way to save our asses. Seeing Ash lying on the ground had affected me, but I knew the risks, and so did he. All of us did, for that matter. Our lives were like a game of Russian roulette. Sometimes you won, sometimes you lost. The unexpected was part of our routine, even when things had been planned carefully.

Suerte slapped me on the back. Then we hugged to celebrate our new collaboration.

"Come on! We have work to do," said Billy.

18

JOE

The call I had received from Lazar worried me. I found it suspicious that he would contact me, as we never had really talked to each other. And when he asked me to gather some emergency medical supplies, I panicked. I had so many questions running through my mind that I needed to take some time to think things through. I asked him about the injury I would have to take care of. He told me it was a gunshot wound.

What the heck!!!

I had seen similar injuries when I worked in the emergency room a few years ago, but it would be another story to perform such an intervention all by myself! I was a nurse, not a doctor! I understood perfectly why they had to stay clear of hospitals. It was obvious this gunshot wound had nothing to do with a hunting accident. Or it was an entirely different type of hunting, as in, a manhunt. I really hoped it wouldn't be too serious. If I couldn't deal with it on my own, what would happen then?

According to Lazar, it would take them less than three hours to arrive. I tried to maximize the time and calm down my nerves. All I could do was contact the only person I knew around here, and I wasn't thrilled about it. He was a famous surgeon from Stonebridge who had accepted a more prestigious position in San Francisco. His name was Adam Jefferson. He was an egomaniac, and I couldn't stand him. On the other hand, he seemed to like me. He often wanted to take me out, but I always turned him down. I thought he was too arrogant for me.

We had sex once or twice, but nothing serious. Loneliness made me do stupid things. He had none of the qualities I was looking for in a man, but I guess he was okay to have sex with now and again.

Considering the situation, my dear Adam seemed to be my only chance. I plucked up the courage to cross the foggy city, as people called it. I barely had the opportunity to admire its beauty. It was only an hour's drive from Monty Valley, and I made a mental note to come back later at a more appropriate time. Having stepped heavily on the gas pedal, I managed to arrive fifteen minutes early. I wasn't used to driving in the city, so I dangerously zigzagged between cars and lanes.

The GPS guided me to St Patrick's Hospital, and when I finally arrived, I ran up the stairs. I realized the choice not to take the elevator made me look suspicious to the staff at the information desk. Next time, I would make sure to use it. I didn't need to attract attention... Luckily, Adam was not in the operating room when I arrived.

Therefore, I could talk to him, even though I had to threaten the secretary to start screaming like a madwoman if she didn't inform him I was there. It was classless, but it was an emergency.

Dr. Jefferson was surprised to see me, but he offered me a cup of coffee. I was restless, but I had to waste those precious minutes to be polite, given what I was about to ask him. When I explained the reason for my visit, which was having access to the pharmacy so I could get some supplies to extract a bullet, he seemed flabbergasted.

Sure, I could've grabbed the tools from a medical supply store, but the real issue was the meds—strong antibiotics and serious painkillers. The kind only a doctor could get his hands on.

It wasn't because I was asking him to break his personal code of ethics...

When I explained the reason for my visit, which was having access to the pharmacy so I could get some supplies to extract a bullet, he seemed flabbergasted.

Sure, I could've grabbed the tools from a medical supply store, but the real issue was the meds—strong antibiotics and serious painkillers. The kind only a doctor could get his hands on.

That wasn't what shocked him, though. Adam was no saint—I knew he wouldn't bat an eye at bending the rules. What really caught him off guard was the fact that I was the one asking.

He'd always said I was a quiet person. What he really meant was boring, I guessed.

He didn't agree to help me right away. I had to beg him, and I was sure he enjoyed every minute of it. Then, the bastard tried to negotiate with me ... I was more or less ready to do anything if my father's life or one of the guys' was in the balance. I felt obliged to do my best to help them. Therefore, I reluctantly accepted an invitation to dinner. As the date was not set, I was counting on not being available.

Time was running out. I had to go. As I was about to leave the hospital with a satchel full of the necessary supplies to perform a minor surgery, Adam showed me the same perfect smile he used to win women over. Unluckily for him, it had no effect on me.

Driving back seemed to take forever, and I felt relieved when I saw the first sand dunes along the road. My heart was beating fast, and I suddenly realized that I hadn't asked who had been hurt. I didn't have the opportunity. Lazar had hung up just after sharing the news with me. He was apparently not the talkative type. Most men were like him around there.

I got out of my Comet and went to the Devil's. Luckily, Mona was already there. She probably had been informed about today's drama. As soon as I walked through the door with my satchel, she jumped on me. I could read in her eyes the same concern I was feeling inside of me.

She grabbed me by the shoulders. "Do you have everything?"

"Yes," I reassured her, panting. "We'll put him on the pool table."

She was gently pulling me by the arm to guide me through the room when I suddenly stopped.

"Who's hurt?" I asked.

"Ash."

"I see..."

I wasn't happy. He or another one of them, it was the same to me. But I couldn't help but be relieved that it wasn't my father. Mona laid a tablecloth on the pool table to protect it, and I opened my satchel to take out what I assumed I would need the most.

"Do you know if... if it's serious? Lazar wasn't very talkative."

"According to Jerry, a bullet grazed his thigh. It's not life-threatening, but driving in a van for three hours isn't helping."

I winced. Nevertheless, I felt relieved by what she had told me. Things would go smoothly unless I messed up. Minutes ticked by, and waiting increased my stress. I stomped. A question came to my mind.

"What do you usually do when something like this happens?" I asked. I realized my stepmom was confused, so I clarified. "I mean, these situations happen... don't they?"

She paused before explaining. "We deal with it. The old doc in town helps us from time to time. But fully trusting someone is not that easy. You have to be very generous, and still... you need to keep an eye on them."

I understood. Living with the fear of being betrayed. The life they chose meant they always had to be on their guard, and they couldn't trust anyone they were doing business with.

"You know," continued Mona, looking absently into the distance. "You should never put your trust in anyone. Especially those who come to the club without being part of it. Sooner or later, they can turn on you for whatever reason and cause you trouble."

I was paying attention to her every word, feeling a bit afraid. I was wondering how they reacted when things like this happened. Would it be the moment for Ash to use his unique talents and save the club from potential threats? The thought made me shiver. Suddenly, we heard a vehicle, which startled us.

"Get ready," Mona encouraged me.

I took a deep breath, trying to overcome the uneasiness that was eating me up inside.

The white van parked right in front of the door, ready to deliver the wounded man. Lazar hastily jumped off and opened the doors. Mona and I rushed to them. I saw Ash lying in the back of the vehicle. He was practically blacked out. In his hand was a half-empty bottle of whiskey. His eyes were half-closed, and his jaw was clenched.

I automatically scrutinized his body to get an idea of how bad things were. Blood was pouring from his right thigh, and he was clumsily holding a bandana soaked in blood on his wound. I recognized it. It was Jerry's. We helped Lazar get the big guy out of the van, but the heavy dead weight was too much for my thin arms. He grumbled as we laid him out on the pool table. In the meantime, Mona was wincing, and she purposely looked away. I slightly lifted the leather torn by the bullet, but the dried blood complicated things. Ash moaned. I saw Mona take a step back. I handed her the flashlight I had in my satchel.

"I need you to point it towards the wound. I need to check it."

Her face suddenly became pale. "What?"

So far, she seemed to be a strong and proud woman, but for the first time since I arrived, she was afraid and lost. Yet, her friend's life was not on the line, at least for now. But if blood kept pouring out for a few more minutes, things could change in a heartbeat.

"What?" I said impatiently.

The tone of my voice was not as soft as I would have liked it to be. Even if I didn't really like this man, I didn't enjoy seeing him in agony. I had never been hit by a bullet, but I would never want to experience that type of pain.

"I am sorry, Sweetheart," Mona said. "I can help you by bringing whatever you need. Towels, water, anything, but I can't stand the sight of blood. I never could. It makes me sick, and I always end up fainting."

I was speechless. I would never have imagined this. The matriarch, who was always bossing people around, couldn't cope with seeing blood. Given the lifestyle she'd chosen, it was somewhat ironic.

"Okay," I said. "Let's get some clean towels, a bowl of fresh water, and a sponge. It will do the trick. Oh, and find other clothes, please, Mona."

Giving orders to my stepmom was awkward, and I would not have dared to do so under other circumstances. In this case, I was guiding her. I had to take matters into my own hands if I wanted things to run smoothly.

"Lazarus?" I caught his attention.

This guy's build intimidated me, as well as his resemblance to a retired pro wrestler, but I had no other choice than to put my fears aside.

"Lazar will do," he said, smiling.

Before I asked, he grabbed the flashlight and pointed it

towards his friend's thigh. It looked terrible. I thanked him with a smile as I realized the wound was deeper than I had expected.

"Could you help me turn him on the other side?" I asked.

"Of course."

Between the two of us, it was a success. To be perfectly honest, I owed it to his steel muscles. My own arms just followed his lead — each person had their own strengths. And I was about to demonstrate mine. I prepared an anesthetic shot. Then I started to cut off his t-shirt after I had freed his arm from his black leather jacket. I threw it away, and it landed softly on the pool table. I stared at the wound that had worried me for the last past hours, but the bullet wasn't lodged inside his thigh. In addition to the laceration, the flesh was torn apart. I sighed as I undid his belt and unbuttoned the top of his jeans to pull it down a little.

"Hey, is the doc undressing me," Ash said. "Or am I dreaming?"

It was so ironic that the man would choose that exact moment to regain consciousness.

"You are dreaming," I joked, not really surprised by his bluntness. "And I am not a doctor, just a nurse. Everyone seems to forget that part."

"Yeah, you're like a mini-doc."

"If you say so."

I made a gesture so Lazar would point the light closer to the wound. He winced when he saw the damage. My patient had his back to us, but he kept on making sick jokes.

"I've always known you wanted to undress me, Mini-doc, but I thought it would be under other circumstances..."

I sighed, annoyed by the man's babbling.

"Can you believe this?" I asked Lazar. "Even after a gunshot wound and half a bottle of whiskey, he is not shutting up ..."

That made his brother-in-arms laugh.

"I am immortal. I'm a Highlander!" the dark-haired man joked.

"Are you positive about that? I can't promise you anything."

He was finally quiet. I started to clean the wound. The anesthesia seemed to work, which was a big relief. What I was about to do would be bad enough. I gave him another shot and waited for a few minutes.

"After all," Ash said. "It's less kinky than I thought it would be."

I repressed a laugh. Lazar too. Even if he was incredibly annoying, I had to admit he was quick on the draw. I had to double-check the full extent of the wound, and what I saw comforted me a little.

"You are lucky. The bullet could have smashed your hip or perforated an organ, but the damage is superficial. It bled a lot, but that's all. I'll have to give you stitches."

I finished cleaning the wound. If we had brought him to a hospital, they would have done a blood transfusion. But I was only a nurse without medical tools in the middle of a bar. He would need some serious rest to get back on his feet.

A loud noise startled me, and I saw, from the corner of

my eye, Mack, Gale, and Bigma come in. They quickly kissed Mona on the cheek. She had retreated behind the counter, watching what I was doing from a distance. Then Casey followed. The little group of men soon stood in a circle around the pool table.

"Hey, Doc, you rock," Mack told me with a wink.

"I'm not a doctor," I repeated, annoyed. "Just a nurse."

"She's a mini-doc," explained Ash before starting to laugh.

Wrong move! The wound had stretched, and he swore between his teeth.

"See how you take advantage of the situation to show your ass to the young and beautiful lady. Always the same dirty old man!" Joked Gale as the men laughed.

I tried to ignore their childish jokes. I had to stitch up the wound, and I needed peace.

"Don't touch my sister," Casey warned.

"We know," Mack replied. "The boss has already lectured us about your sis."

"He's smart!" said my younger brother.

I chuckled before regaining my composure. "And now, guys, get out. I need to stay focused. I wouldn't want to give him crooked stitches."

No one moved.

"Get out!" Ash hollered.

He had more authority than I did. It worked, but the guys couldn't resist teasing him a little bit more. They probably enjoyed the fact that he couldn't fight back.

Hanger and Foxy joined the others, and they all gathered around Mona. I heard them laugh and caught a few morbid jokes, but I didn't really pay attention. I was getting used to it. If I had been taking care of another one of them, things might have been different. In the case of Ash, he seemed to be a loud-mouth and a hothead with an oversized ego. When you put all these traits in one person, you get the king of explosives.

I was working on the first stitches when my father hastily walked in, followed by Billy. They came right to me with fear in their eyes.

"Ash, my bro, are you okay?" asked Jerry.

"It could be worse," he whispered, laughing.

The Wild Crows' big boss turned around and gave me a quizzical look, full of gratitude.

"Is he going to be alright?"

"Yes," I reassured him. "He's fortunate. The wound is superficial. The bullet did some damage, but it didn't touch any vital parts of his body. In two or three months, all you'll see is a scar. The only problem is that he won't be able to ride his motorcycle for a few weeks."

"Girls love scars!" said the drunken man as I finished stitching him up.

My father chuckled.

"Frankenstein would agree," joked Billy.

"A general anesthesia would have been indicated in this case," I grumbled.

"Thanks," whispered my father in a serious voice.

I realized my intervention had saved him. I could feel his gratitude.

"You're welcome," I replied.

It was sincere. If I could help, I would do it. It was in my nature, and when it came to my father's life, I didn't want to judge. All I wanted was to be a part of it if he was ready to let me.

I finished stitching up my patient while Jerry called the others for a meeting. They disappeared upstairs.

"What's upstairs?" I asked him.

"The room."

"The room?" I repeated.

"Yeah, the table at which your father presides is up there."

"Is this the room where you hold the club's meetings?"

"Yes, ma'am. And no women are allowed."

I paused, reflecting on how they kept men and women apart. It seemed to be part of their lifestyle. I decided not to give it too much thought, even though I found it weird.

"And we're done," I said, wiping my hands on a clean towel. "At least, I am."

Ash buttoned his pants, and I helped him fasten his belt, as it was painful for him to bend over. Then, he tried to get up, but it was too complicated. I was about to ask Mona for help, but I realized she had vanished. So, I offered him my shoulder. It was better than nothing. When he sat on the pool table, I took a step back, but he grabbed my wrist, wincing. Even the smallest gesture seemed painful, and even though he was quite annoying, I was touched.

"Thanks, Mini-doc. You killed it."

"You're welcome," I said after spending a few seconds trying to figure out his real thoughts in vain. "You need rest. You've lost a lot of blood. Stay here until the others come down. They will help you out."

"No, I'll be fine. I'm a rock."

He was back to his old self. I tried to dissuade him, but he was as stubborn as a mule. He tried to get back on his feet. He managed to stand up for two seconds. As soon as he tried to walk, he collapsed. I had the reflex to push him back on the pool table before he slid down too low. I would never have been able to lift him by myself. I helped him sit and left him there. His eyes were glassy. Exhaustion was getting the best of him. I only hoped he hadn't lost too much blood. He would need to be monitored during the next few hours. That was just my luck! At least I didn't have to argue with him to make him lay on his back. He was so weak that he did it naturally.

The rock was a man, after all, but I kept quiet.

19

JERRY

Casey was the last one to enter the room. He closed the door behind him and sat around the table with us. I slammed my gavel on the wooden surface so the meeting would officially start. Everyone was there except for Ash. He had tried to overdo it, and now he had to deal with the consequences. It was just like him. He was always pushing things. On the other hand, his little handmade device had worked perfectly. His taste for danger didn't undermine his talents in the other fields.

"So, first things first. Ash was shot today. Don't fret, he is fine. He's out of the woods. He won't be able to ride a bike for a few weeks, but everything will be back to normal soon. Now, he needs to rest to get better. If I could get two volunteers to take him back home after this meeting, that would be great."

"I'll take care of it," said Billy, raising his hand.

"I'm with you," added Hanger.

"Okay, Perfect! Now, let's get serious. We managed to convince the Bandoleros to do business with us. They have ordered two hundred Glocks and a hundred M4s that need to be delivered by next month."

I could read joy on my men's faces, and I enjoyed witnessing it.

"Bigma. You call Callum."

He didn't protest. He knew he had to make up for his mistake. It would be a good way to test him. After the other day's fiasco, he had to redeem himself.

"And what about the Russians?" Foxy asked impatiently.

I kept my eyes fixed on him to keep all of them in suspense. Then, I got caught in the game and started to laugh out loud, thinking about today's victory. Billy got drawn in by my euphoria, followed by Lazar. Our hilarity was probably due to post-traumatic stress.

"So?" asked Casey.

With effort, I managed to regain my composure.

"Bam!" screamed Lazar.

Once again, we laughed out loud. We all did, and when I heard Foxy say "Bam" in a puzzled voice, I nodded.

"Bam. Game over."

"All of them?" he asked anxiously.

His question calmed things down. I cleared my throat before resuming my role. "No. Sergei and a few of his men."

"Do you know what it means?" asked Hanger with concern.

"Yes, I do. His brother will seek revenge."

Those few words were enough to bring us back to reality. Retaliation wasn't just a game to the Russians—it was an art form honed to perfection in the highest-stakes arena. When they struck back, they didn't just play in the big leagues; they owned the field.

"We need to be alert," whispered Billy. "Don't let your loved one's out of your sight. There is no need to be paranoid, but we have to be careful."

"Let's wait for him to make the first move. He'll come for sure. And we will welcome him properly," I declared to everyone.

My plan seemed to be approved unanimously.

"With the quantities ordered by the Mexicans, we'll get out of debt. And if they are satisfied, they might do business with us again."

Everyone nodded, and I knew my men were thinking the same thing. The sinews of war were money. None of us was rolling in it. Our lifestyle gave us freedom, but there was a price to pay. Our future was always uncertain, especially when it came to safety or finances. One had to get their hands dirty to earn a decent living. All of us were ready, with our sleeves rolled up to our elbows, waiting to seize any opportunity that fate would throw our way.

"If you don't have any further questions, that will be all for tonight. And I remind you that our wounded friend is waiting for his ride."

As I was about to slam the hammer three times to end the meeting, Gale raised his hand.

"I have something to tell you."

His unexpected intervention caught everyone's attention. All eyes turned to him, and he suddenly seemed uneasy.

"As you know, I got out of jail because I gave away one of the Kasabovs' storage places. The one that's close to Hornett."

We all acknowledged, eager to hear the whole story. My senses told me that some kind of dodgy business was going on. Another potential source of problems was coming my way. Gale rubbed his hands together before he spoke.

"And I got a lighter sentence for good behavior."

"Get to the point," I encouraged him.

"Yeah. Okay. So, let's say that I didn't run into any trouble at Karson, thanks to some guys who ... protected me."

I knew something was going on, and I was about to hear the full story.

"Come on, tell us," I ordered him. "Who protected you?"

"The Black Wolves."

Everyone stayed perfectly silent around the table. The Black Wolves had decided to protect Gale. It was just crazy. Personally, I knew every corner of Karson, Monty Valley's county jail, like the back of my hand, so I had a fair idea of how things worked over there. Groups were formed according to ethnicity. That's how things worked. It was an unspoken code. The black community stuck together, white men formed another group, and the Mexicans kept to themselves. Besides them, smaller groups emerged, all led by strong-headed men with dubious pasts and mouths as big as their egos.

Therefore, learning that the Wolves from San Francisco took a Monty Valley Caucasian man under their wing was hard to swallow. Especially when Gale had been convicted because of our line of business.

So why did they help him? They didn't do it out of the goodness of their heart or without any second thoughts. I could be a rather nice man–from time to time–but I was no fool. We had sold them large quantities of drugs some time ago, but since then, we had stopped dealing. We were not in contact anymore. They had their own suppliers as far as weapons were concerned. They dealt with the Chinese, and they had nothing to do with us anymore.

"Why?"

I was so tense that it was the only word I could pronounce.

Gale seemed uneasy. I knew I wasn't going to like what was coming next. I was so damn sure of it.

"Without them, the Kasabovs' henchmen would have stabbed me on day one. I owe them."

"What did they want in return?"

"I didn't ask for anything," replied Gale without answering my question. "They saved my life, and I didn't have a choice. I had to make a deal with them."

This guy was going to kill me softly by retaining information! He must have sensed my impatience as he finally spilled the beans.

"They made sure I would survive in there, and all they want in return is a little help from the outside. The feds have a case on them. Cops are about to find their hideout in Richmond. They want us to clear it before they find the drugs."

I almost choked as anger rose through my body. I briefly lost control, unable to refrain from hitting the wooden table with a raging fist.

"Fuck, you are an idiot!"

"I didn't have a choice!" he defended himself. "Otherwise, I would have been stabbed by a Russian inmate, Jerry!"

I grumbled and found the strength to overcome my anger.

"Eighty kilos," Gale added.

I sighed, completely overwhelmed by the bad news. We all looked at each other. I realized some of my men were surprised, while others seemed annoyed and disappointed. The decision had been taken around this same table. We had agreed to stop everything after Gale's conviction. It had been more than four years now since the club had stopped selling drugs and switched to arms trafficking. One risky business was more than enough, and rifles were less addictive than cocaine. I let out a grumble.

"They want us to move eighty kilos for them?" I repeated incredulously.

"Yeah."

Gale's voice was only a murmur. Despite his military look with his blond crew haircut and his large forehead, he seemed scared. "They're waiting to hear from us soon."

I took a few moments to think about the situation. Did we really have a choice? A debt was a debt, and it had to be paid to avoid a war between clubs.

"You go and call Davis Brown. When you agree on a

date, come and tell me about it. We'll talk about the logistics later."

He nodded.

"Well, any other bad news we need to discuss tonight?"

Billy started to laugh in the corner of the room. I couldn't keep my anger to myself when I talked to the guys, but no one dared to speak up. It was better like this. I had to keep my authority intact, even after twelve years of presiding over this assembly. I grabbed the hammer and closed the meeting. I'd had enough for the night.

They all left the room, but I held Gale behind. I waited a few moments so we would be alone.

"Keep an eye on Mack," I said. "He can't be trusted around blow."

"Alright," whispered Gale.

"Old demons are tenacious."

"We all have a past, Jerry. Try to trust him a little bit. He's a good guy."

"I agree," I said. "But I also know him and how bad things were at the time. We'd better keep a close eye on him, especially during this drug transfer."

"Don't worry. I'll take care of it."

Gale patted my shoulder, and we exchanged a friendly look.

"Thanks, Jerry. And...I am really sorry."

"Get the hell out of here," I ordered with a half-smile.

When I returned to the ground floor, Mona was waiting for me on a stool. I went directly to her to give her a kiss before turning my attention to the pool table. Billy and Hanger were carrying a half-asleep Ash.

Just behind them was my daughter with a satchel full of medical supplies and medicines. She had dealt with the critical situation way better than I expected. Performing such surgery was a lot to ask for. And without a moment's hesitation, she'd taken up the challenge. I knew that she'd done it for me, and I felt slightly guilty about using her to fix our mistakes. But there she was, slowly finding her place in my hectic life. It was priceless.

The guys walked past me, and I gave a wink at my old friend, Ash.

"Next time, try to be smart," I joked.

"What do you know about drama?" grumbled the dark-haired man. "Thanks to my little show, they were convinced the weapons were in the truck."

"Yeah, right. You are a misunderstood artist," joked Billy, who was carrying a man weighing half his own weight.

The three of us laughed, bonded by an undeniable friendship.

"Come on, rest for a while, Bro. You need it."

Without another word, they took him to the van parked in the workshop. Mona opened the door for them. When I saw Joe getting in her car, I stopped her.

"Are you going with them?"

"Yes, I cannot let him out of my sight. He's lost too much blood. I can't be a hundred percent sure he's going to be alright. I need to monitor him while his body recovers. If anything goes wrong, I need to be next to him."

"Going to a hospital is not an option," I warned her, still feeling grateful for her devoted care.

"I know that. But I have a trick upon my sleeve. Just in case..." she whispered.

Joe didn't say anything else, but I was sure she wasn't bluffing. I smiled at her and kissed her on her forehead.

"Thanks for everything," I said.

I watched her walk away into the night, fully aware that an angel had just entered my complicated life.

20

JOE

I followed the van with my Comet, driving south in the dark night. About fifteen minutes later, we reached a quiet neighborhood. I parked next to Hanger and Billy in front of a small bungalow. I turned off the engine and joined the three bikers. They were walking Ash to the front door.

"Keys?" asked Billy.

"In my jacket pocket."

With a sigh, the stubbiest guy of all got the bunch of keys and opened the way to the den of a wolf named Trevor. The big, tall, dark-haired man shot me an amused glance.

"So, gonna be my chaperone tonight?"

"I don't really have a choice," I grumbled. "I wouldn't want your death on my conscience."

He repressed a laugh, probably because his healing wound hurt him badly.

"It works for me. Maybe I should get shot more often. But I'm not sure my wife would like that."

I froze. No one had ever mentioned he had a wife. Maybe he also had a bunch of kids. How would I explain my being there without giving any details? A flood of questions came to my tired mind. Did they know about his life at the club? His wife would probably not tolerate my presence there all night long. It would make sense. Why had I believed these men were lonesome cowboys? After all, Billy and Jerry had women in their lives, so why would it be different for Ash? He was apparently a bit crazy, but he was handsome, even with his twisted mind and insufferable behavior.

Then they laughed, and I understood. Once more, I had been the victim of their crude humor. I didn't say anything, and I entered the house. The subdued lighting revealed wooden furniture. Their color matched the beams. There were also two big sofas, a large TV screen, a coffee table, and, in the back, a kitchenette. The guys stepped into the corridor, but Ash stopped them.

"No, leave me on the couch. I don't have a TV in my room. I am going to freak out if I can't move."

A second later, the two heavily built men laid their pal down on the largest sofa in the living room. I almost found it touching when Billy placed the pillow behind the wounded man's head.

"Hanger!" yelled Ash. "Can you grab a quilt for me from the hall closet?"

He left right away and brought back a woolen throw that he spread on his friend's legs.

"Can you also remove my boots?"

With a roll of his eyes, Billy sighed and took care of it himself.

"If you could massage my feet, guys, I would be in paradise," joked the big guy before laughing out loud. "And if I need to pee, who do I call?"

Billy threw a towel at his face and laughed, too.

"You hold it!"

Ash was lying on his side. The outrageous, clumsy guy was in agony. I could tell by the look on his pale face. He played the part of the indestructible tough guy perfectly, and it was not that far from the truth. But there was something off. I could tell.

"See you, old pal," Billy said. "And be a gentleman with Joe. It's rather nice of her to look after you tonight."

"I can behave, Bro. Who do you think you're talking to?"

His horrified expression made us all laugh. Then, Billy talked to me in a more serious tone. With his round cheeks and his long, gray, shaggy hair, he looked like an alien. Goodness emanated from him, something like ancestral wisdom. I liked this man. He seemed to be a key person in the club, and I understood what my father had seen in him when he recruited him. He was a father figure, the kind of guy capable of keeping his cool during a storm.

"We're gonna be on our way, Joe. If there's anything, call us."

I politely nodded. Jerry had already gone through the trouble of texting me the list of the club members' phone numbers. It would probably be useful sooner or later. The two bodyguards left, and I suddenly felt isolated inside this wounded bear's cave, especially since I didn't know him very well.

He leaned towards the table to grab the remote, and then he switched on the TV.

"There are more bedspreads in the closet if you need them."

I nodded and went to get one. When I returned to the living room, Ash seemed to have chosen a TV program. I sat on the second couch and watched the show. It featured musicians who had found fame in the sixties and seventies, mainly during the Woodstock era.

"Janis Joplin, that's real music," said my new room-mate, watching the screen with admiration in his eyes.

Surprised, I observed him. The painkillers seemed to get him high. The sofas formed a right angle so that I could look right into his face.

"My mom loved her," I whispered.

"Cosmic Mama. It was her nickname. Damn, that woman really had balls. I was born a little bit too late," he complained jokingly. "Too bad. We would have made a wonderful duo, she and I."

I repressed a smile.

"A hippie crafting bomb mechanism," I said. "That would have been unheard of."

"Would you believe it if I told you I was a rolling stone?"

I shrugged. "I see you more as a veteran than a militant of the *Peace and Love* movement," I told him.

Ash raised an eyebrow in surprise.

"Some of us are vets, that's right. But we don't believe in all that shit anymore. The others don't even speak about it. And politics would hurt the club. I was in the army for only two years. Wasn't really working for me, following orders and all this shit."

"Come to think of it, it makes sense."

"Suck up to a colonel, no thanks. And we are always on the road. In the club, we don't give a shit about laws and conventions ..."

"Drifters," I concluded, feeling amused.

"Janice would have been proud!"

I laughed again—Was it becoming a habit? Underneath their leather jackets, they were full of surprises, and some were good. The famous singer's voice played in my head, and I rediscovered the sweetness of the tones from my childhood memories. Approximately ten minutes later, I felt Ash's gaze on me. I felt uneasy, even though I couldn't see anything threatening in his eyes, only curiosity.

"Do you really intend to check up on me all night, Mini-doc?" he asked.

"That's the plan."

"Then you're gonna need some coffee."

He paused as if another idea had crossed his mind. "Or a beer?"

"Coffee is fine," I answered, winking at him. "I don't handle alcohol very well.

My answer seemed to amuse him, and he grabbed his thigh again. Maybe he recalled my recent performance at the club.

"In the kitchen, next to the fridge. And I'd like a beer..."

I stood up and went to pour myself a hot cup of coffee. When I came back to the living room, I had brought back a big glass of water for my patient. He shot me a nasty look before giving me a pout.

"Nurse's orders, just water tonight."

He grumbled but accepted the drink I was offering him. I went back to the sofa and got comfortable, pulling the spread over my legs. I grabbed my phone and programmed regular alarms, one every two hours. My roommate wasn't going to appreciate it, but it was necessary. I was no machine. My phone would help me remember my duty.

"How do you feel?" I asked.

"Fine, except I feel like a part of my leg has been torn apart."

"You're not far from the truth... If you need to sleep, don't mind me. Pretend I'm not here. Rest will be the best of medicines if you want to recover rapidly."

"Don't worry, Mini-doc. It should not be long now. My old body isn't as resistant as it used to be."

Even if it was said as a joke, something in his voice moved me.

"And how old is this body exactly?"

"That's impolite."

I looked him up and down, trying to make him understand that I was not buying his sudden shyness. Not me!

"Forty-nine, young lady."

I paused. I thought he was fifty. I was not so far from the truth. His fashion style made him look younger, but his face was scarred and wrinkled, which gave away his age.

"Not too bad for your age," I said.

My joke worked. He was smiling again. "Thanks, Kiddo."

"You're mistaken. I am not a kid."

"You are to me."

"I am twenty-seven," I said defiantly.

"That's what I said."

He had the last word, and I decided to stop this playful exchange, even though it was friendly. My patient needed rest. I wasn't there to keep him awake with my questions. When I saw his eyelids flutter, I went back to the fridge, where I had seen a flyer for a Mexican restaurant with delivery service. I took the phone and called The Conqueror. I ordered two taco combos. It wasn't exactly healthy food, but if he woke up hungry during the night, he'd have something to eat.

The delivery boy knocked on the door half an hour later, and I gave him a generous tip. The smell of the chili sauce was enough to wake up the tall, dark-haired man, even though he was sound asleep.

"One point for you, Mini-doc."

Without a word, I handed him one of the boxes. He straightened his back a little bit and devoured its content. Eating was good for him. Between two bites, I felt my phone vibrate.

Jerry: If you have any problems, I'm a phone call away. Your dad.

Such thoughtfulness made me smile. He could have signed "Daddy," but I assumed he was still feeling a bit uneasy about our relationship. I could understand it, as I thought the same. I answered it immediately.

Me: It's all good. Thanks, and see you tomorrow. Your daughter.

I could have just signed "Joe," but the line he had unconsciously thrown to me was too tempting. Undoubtedly, his next message would be signed "Daddy," which was such a beautiful, proud, and majestic word written with a capital letter. I was hopeful. My mischievous smile must have sparked my patient's interest. As he was eating his taco, he started to fish for information.

"Back to business, Mini-doc?"

"Stop it with this stupid nickname," I warned him, putting my phone away. "I hate it, and it doesn't make any sense."

"That's exactly why I like it. So, who is worried for you?"

"My dad."

"No kidding? Jerry playing the doting father, I would never have believed it. He was sort of affectionate with your brother, but with you, it's different. A girl needs more protection, especially with our lifestyle..."

"I can understand that. The way you consider women is... peculiar."

My words surprised Ash, who had stopped eating. "What do you mean?"

I tried to carefully choose my words to avoid any misunderstanding. I found it hard to find the right words, especially on delicate matters.

"Let's say that women have it tough at the club."

"I disagree. It's a deal. They take care of us, and in return, we protect them."

His opinion on the male-female relationship inside the club surprised me. Evidently, he saw things differently.

"Being a sweetie is rather... humiliating to me. However, they seem satisfied with their fate," I said.

Ash frowned, seemingly puzzled by my explanation.

"What do you mean by humiliating?"

"You consider them as your property, items for your pleasure. You ..." I took a few seconds to choose my words carefully. "You use them whenever you want. All they have to do is obey."

"They made a choice. No one forced them," Ash said defensively.

"I know that. But what I don't understand is why they are okay with it."

"They want our protection."

"But they aren't in harm's way if they don't hang out with you. They could have more freedom outside, but they choose to stay."

A strange smile appeared in his dark beard. "They want to be with bikers. That's why they stay around."

"And every night they act as escorts..."

"And for free!" he added.

I laughed, not feeling as annoyed as I thought I would be.

"I don't know. It's always been this way," he said evasively. "They are part of the game, and they belong to our world. They love bad boys. It turns them on, and we are happy to get a hearty welcome when we come back after a shitty day."

I reflected on his words and came to the conclusion

that it was a specificity of their world. Maybe atypical and marginal characters behaved like this.

"It's probably the jacket," I joked.

"The tattoos and guns, as well. The whole package!"

This time, I laughed wholeheartedly, and it felt liberating.

"I imagine they all hope to become a regular, just like Mona."

"Yeah, I guess. It doesn't often happen, though. Our lifestyle isn't compatible with the picture-perfect family cliché. We don't take anything for granted. Things can go south in a heartbeat. We never know how long we're gonna be on this earth and if we are going to be able to bring home enough dough to take care of a woman and kids. We are like this casino game, roulette. Many players, many losers."

I was listening to him carefully, and his metaphor struck a chord.

"But Jerry seems to lead a pretty steady life despite his role."

"That's because Mona has accepted it. She's the best! She's ready to sacrifice a lot for the club, you know. A true lady."

"Like Janis," I joked.

"Yeah, like Janis," said Ash, smiling.

I finished my taco and wiped my mouth before continuing with my questions.

"Billy seems to be doing okay too. I mean, he's in a stable relationship..."

"I guess you can say that, but Beckie would like him to retire... Billy joined the club when it was formed. It's his whole life. It would be easier to put a square peg in a round hole than to make him quit. They fight a lot about this. I enjoy peace!"

Ash was a lone wolf. Men like him seemed to be the norm in the Wild Crows. Feelings weren't a part of their lives.

"Have you ever been married?"

"Very nosy," he joked. "And inappropriate."

"This word doesn't suit you, Ash."

"Okay," he surrendered. "I was married for four years. The story is a common one... high-school sweethearts, illusions, and constant arguments about the club."

So, the king of explosives had a stable life once upon a time. The club seemed to devour anything that belonged to a normal life. It came before everything else. Brotherhood was their priority.

"Do you have kids?"

"Is this a formal interrogation, Lieutenant Joe?"

I laughed.

"Is that my new nickname?"

"You kinda asked for it."

"No," I said.

"No, what?"

"It's not an interrogation. I just like to know who I'm talking with. From the outside, you seem very mysterious," I explained. "I have always liked to figure out things that seem complicated at first sight instead of dealing with clear-cut situations."

"If you say so... Thanks for the compliment."

"I'm not sure it was one, but you are welcome."

"No, no kids," Ash said at last. "That I know of."

I nodded, feeling satisfied to have gathered some privileged information on the mysterious Ash.

"How about you, Miss Detective? What do you have to confess?"

"Absolutely nothing."

"No husband or kids?"

"There's none of that in my life," I said almost regretfully. "And no, I am not here to seduce men dressed in leather jackets!"

He burst out laughing.

"Still," he started between two sips of water, "I'm pretty sure I saw Mack leaving your place last week."

I was speechless. I had to admit the way I had kicked him out of my apartment wasn't super smart. Anyone could have seen him, and apparently, Ash had. I had to face the consequences.

"You're not quite as insightful as Columbo," I said.

"Really?"

"Really! To tell you the whole story, the morning after the party organized to celebrate Gale's return, I found this idiot fast asleep on my couch when I woke up. He said my door was unlocked, which meant he felt entitled to enter my place or something like that. And that's why you saw him leave in the morning. I threw him out. I am not one of those girls."

After taking a few seconds to think about what I had just told him, Ash burst out laughing.

"What an ass!" He laughed. "He is a punk!"

"On a positive note, I haven't heard from him since then."

"He got the message loud and clear."

"I hope so," I said.

"He is a good guy when you get to know him."

"Maybe with his 'bros.'" I air quoted. "I'm a woman, it's totally different."

Ash smirked. "He tried his luck and lost. Mack is not used to being turned down."

"None of you are," I corrected him.

I had a point. Ash's mouth froze in an "o" as he took the blow.

He laughed. "You may be right."

"I am right," I corrected him with a smile. "I haven't been around for a long time. The new girl on the block effect will wear off."

Ash put his taco wrapping on the table and looked at me silently for a minute. "You're just like your father."

I didn't know how I should interpret his words. Coming from one of his closest friends, they were surely meant to be nice. The Canned Heat sang *"On the Road Again,"* and we fell silent to listen to their lively music.

21

JOE

I couldn't stand the damn alarm anymore, but it was necessary. I still had to get up one more time. I would be the last medical check before sunrise. My eyelids were heavy, and I turned my head towards the couch while I turned the alarm off. I must have had four hours of sleep if I totaled all the phases. The day was going to be rough. I could sense it.

When I discovered the couch was empty, I panicked.

"Ash?" I called.

A cracking sound startled me. I got up to my feet so fast that I felt lightheaded for a second.

"Ash, are you there?"

I rushed to the corridor, thinking something terrible might have happened when I was fast asleep. Then I saw him. He was leaning against the wall after closing one of the doors.

"Hi, Baby Girl!"

I couldn't care less about the new nickname he had given me. I was so relieved to see him alive. When my heart rate started to slow down, I realized that it might have missed a beat or two.

"You scared the hell out of me. You could have woken me up if you need to get up. Just in case..."

He looked at my face and then laughed. "You wanted to help me take a piss?"

It took me a moment to understand what he had told me, as my brain was still not fully awake. I winced.

"No, but if you had woken me up, I could have waited for you in the living room to be ready if you fell."

"You wouldn't be able to lift me back to my feet on your own."

"No, but I could have called for help. Your body is still weak. It wouldn't take much for you to faint, believe me."

He nodded, and I assumed he was joking.

"Come on, idiot," I said.

I let him lean on me so he could walk back to the sofa. I poured two coffees and put his down on the coffee table. I saw gratitude in his eyes.

"So, what's today's plan?" he asked me cheerfully.

"That's a good question. I can hardly imagine myself following you around all day long. But on the other hand, it'd be best if I could keep an eye on you for a few more hours. A sudden move or a violent effort, and you'll fall to the ground..."

"I get it," he interrupted me, waving his hand. "So, are you coming with me?"

"I guess so. I imagine we are not going very far, given your state."

"I feel perfectly fine. Don't underestimate me, young lady."

A smile came across my face, and I let him talk.

"Let's go to the Devil's Trip. I might not be useful, but I have no intention of staying here all day long, slumped on the couch."

I was about to dissuade him, but I could read the determination on his face. I knew it would be a lost battle. He was a difficult man to negotiate with. He was twenty years older than me, and he was stubborn as a mule.

"Have I just been promoted to private chauffeur?" I joked.

"Yep. On the bright side, it won't be the two of us anymore. You will be able to run errands."

He was right.

"Okay, let's go to the Devil's."

The irony of the phrase wasn't lost on me.

A broad smile appeared in the man's beard.

As expected, Ash couldn't behave himself during the fifteen minutes it took us to drive from his place to the workshop. He had to touch everything inside my old Comet and asked tons of weird questions. He had this crazy, unpredictable, and hyper behavior. If you added a certain outspokenness and offbeat humor, you got a bizarre mix, almost as explosive as the charges he prepared for the club.

For a few moments, I pictured him crafting a home-made bomb, and I laughed uncontrollably, visualizing a mad scientist. I knew it wasn't funny, as it was a violent act, but I couldn't help myself. Imagining him with his curly and uncontrollable hair, his darting gaze, and an imaginary white lab coat was hilarious. He asked me why I was laughing so hard, but I didn't tell. Instead, I enjoyed watching his frustration when he didn't get a straight answer. He was so used to getting his way.

I parked in the main parking lot, which was still empty. I saw a customer in the workshop. Lazar was talking to her. As I was helping Ash out of the car, the big, tall guy with long gray hair came to my rescue.

"So, how is the patient doing?" Lazar asked.

"Perfectly fine," Ash answered proudly.

"As long as he's talking, we know he's breathing," I joked.

Lazar smiled and walked with us to the Devil's. It was closed at that hour, but Mona had left a set of keys under a flowerpot, and she had sent me a text message to let me know about it. I opened the door, and the two bikers followed me inside. I served them coffee as they sat on stools at the end of the counter. It must have been uncomfortable for Ash, but after all, he was old enough to make his own decision.

I sent a text message to my father to let him know we were there. Foxy joined us. He was happy to find the Devil's trip open so early in the day. He was wearing overalls, and his hands were covered in motor oil. I assumed he'd been working at the workshop that morning.

Was my father paying them by the hour, or was their compensation part of the other activities of the club? No, it was impossible. It would raise a red flag for the IRS. He had to give them a pay slip. Did they have a schedule, or were some of them exempted? I made a mental note to get to the bottom of that later. They say curiosity killed the cat, but that was just me. I couldn't help it.

"So?" asked the redheaded man. "Did you have to take care of him all night?"

Two loud laughs sliced the air.

"Someone had to do it. You owe me one," I said, winking at Ash, who was grumbling to himself. Then, a Harley and a bright red SUV appeared in the distance.

"The bosses are here," Lazar said.

They had been fast. Their houses couldn't have been more than a few minutes away. My father arrived first and greeted the guys with a sudden hand wave before kissing me on the forehead. Mona was just behind him, and she kissed everyone. She was more affectionate with the man that the others had nicknamed the "survivor," and Ash couldn't resist playing the victim to get sympathy from the boss' wife. It was a pretty smart move. At last, she greeted me.

"Are you okay?" asked my father with concern in his voice.

"Just tired, but I am fine. Mission accomplished, Boss. No casualties."

He laughed, and I served them coffee. That's when it dawned on me.

"Why don't you open the bar during the day? It could be a place where the workshop's customers waited. It would be a total change from the people that come at night."

"What's wrong with the ones that come at night?" he asked, surprised.

"Nothing. I was just saying we could work longer hours to attract more customers."

Mona, who was listening attentively, nodded her head. "Your daughter is right..."

My father rubbed his forehead pensively before speaking out. "The concept was always to run a night bar..."

"So what?" asked Mona. "We can do both. Joe is right. If we open during the day, we'll get more customers. At the end of the afternoon or a bit later, our regular customers will slowly replace the new ones. Change of people, change of atmosphere. We'll get used to it. I think it's worth trying."

Mona rephrasing my words changed everything. She knew the family business and its customers perfectly. Therefore, she knew the kind of opportunity it represented. Jerry seemed to take the idea more seriously.

"We would need to hire staff. Right now, we can't afford it."

"Don't consider it as an expense. It's an investment," I added. "And you can ask some of the sweeties to help in the beginning. Then, when it's viable, you'll hire a third person."

The power couple looked at each other quizzically, and everyone around was waiting for their decision.

"I need to think about it," Jerry concluded.

Mona gave me a broad smile full of promises. She would surely talk to him privately. After a few minutes, Jerry reminded Lazar and Foxy that they were not paid to sit at the bar, and I got the information I was looking for. The two men nodded and left in a flash.

Mona followed them to take care of the workshop's accounting, which she was responsible for. I admired her. Not only was she working long hours at the bar, but she also managed all the paperwork related to the workshop. She worked really hard on top of being the motherly figure of the club.

I was now alone with my father and Ash.

"Well," blurted my father. "Mona's gone, and I wanted to tell you something."

His right-hand man and I looked at him silently, waiting for him to speak out. "Mona doesn't want anybody to know, but she's turning fifty tomorrow."

"No way!" I said.

I was surprised, and my father noticed it.

"You're so lucky to be the man of such a gorgeous fifty-year-old woman," I said, poking him gently.

He looked at me and smiled at me sweetly. "That's right. I'm a lucky man."

"Absolutely," laughed Ash.

"So," Jerry continued. "I wanted to organize a special celebration at my place tomorrow night."

"With the members of the club?" asked the tall, dark-haired man.

"Yeah, all the guys," he added. "I'll eventually ask the regulars and the kids to join us."

"Good idea," I said.

Ash just nodded.

"I am counting on you to pass the word around. Let's say eight o'clock sharp. And not a word to Mona. She has no idea..."

I smiled at him in childish anticipation, deeply moved by his feelings for his wife. Both my father and Mona were good-looking and as passionately in love as a young couple. Suddenly, a question crossed my mind.

"And where do you live?" I asked.

Jerry laughed.

"Things got so intense since you arrived that I didn't get a chance to invite you home. Shame on me."

I put a reassuring hand on his shoulder. "You've welcomed me with open arms and an open heart. All's good, trust me!"

I suddenly realized what Ash had meant the day before. My father was very protective, even though I had just arrived. He already loved me. I was his daughter, and he was my father. Time wouldn't change that. It was engraved in our hearts as an undeniable truth from the day we met.

"Come and pick me up. I'll give you directions," said Ash.

Amused and touched by my father's thoughtfulness, I observed him.

"And you, don't try to take advantage of the situation," Jerry warned nicely.

"You know me, Bro. I'm not like that."

"It depends on the girl we're talking about!" retorted my father.

"She's your daughter, for god's sake. You know you can trust me!"

I let them talk and laughed to myself. The place was not busy, so I left and started to clean the back room before the scheduled delivery arrived at noon. I emptied a few boxes before throwing them out, but I had to stop as the lack of sleep was weighing on me. I perched on a keg and leaned back against the wall.

A loud knocking startled me. I immediately straightened and rubbed my eyes, realizing I had fallen asleep in the back room. I returned to the bar and saw my father at the door.

"We were worried," he said.

The next second, he and his friend were laughing out loud. My lethargic behavior had betrayed me, and they easily guessed why I hadn't returned sooner. I yawned and stretched like a cat. Jerry handed me a cup of strong coffee. I really needed it. I looked at Ash. He seemed fine. That's what mattered the most to me, and it made me forget about my own fatigue. Instinctively, I hugged my father, who wasn't expecting it. Then, I pulled myself together and left without a look back.

"I really need a shower," I said. "And at least two hours of sleep! He's all yours."

I was no monster, so I planted a kiss on his prickly gray beard. Then, I looked at him sweetly and gave him my most beautiful smile. Thinking only about the comfort of my bed, I winked at my patient and left. I didn't even complain about the three flights of stairs. I ran up, called by an irresistible melody that promised me sweet and relaxing dreams. Finally, I could rest.

The boss and his right-hand man owed it to me.

22

JOE

It was almost 7:00 p.m. when I parked in front of Trevor's house. It had a cozy feel with its dim lights coming through the windows. I knocked on the door, but I didn't wait for an answer. I walked in before Ash could get up so he wouldn't do any unnecessary movement.

"Hi," I greeted him.

As I expected, I found him lying on the couch. His face seemed more relaxed than the day before. I was so relieved to see that he was getting better by the minute.

"Hi," he replied wearily.

"No nickname today?"

"I can't think of any right now. Don't worry. It'll come back."

"I am not worried one bit!" I replied with a smile. I walked around the sofa to stand in front of him. "I came early because I wanted to check if the wound was infected before we go."

"I don't think so. You are a pro! And the pills you gave me worked."

I noticed he had tried to dress nicely for Mona's birthday party that evening. He had replaced his old t-shirt with a fitted black shirt and a pair of well-cut jeans that looked nicer than his traditional black pants. I also noticed he had sprayed himself with a spicy cologne. Ash looked like a new man, and I appreciated the efforts he had made. It was a tribute to the love he felt for Mona and Jerry.

"Can I check?" I asked.

"Yeah, of course."

"Anyway, it's time to change your bandage."

I sat beside him, and he let me do my work. I lifted his shirt, and I ripped off the bandage as carefully as I could. I couldn't see any swelling or abnormal redness. I felt relieved. The hazardous surgery I had performed in a bar seemed to be a success.

"So?" he asked.

I could sense his concern.

"It looks fine."

"I told you," he replied happily.

I opened my satchel and started to clean the healing wound. When I was done, I dressed it with a new bandage. I had to be careful. Having taken care of such a serious injury on a pool table was insane!

After putting all my stuff away, I stood up and offered him my hand. "Let's go, champion!"

He gave me a shy smile and grabbed my arm to stand up. His walking was more assured, and he didn't need any help when he was going at his own pace. His stitches and skin seemed to stretch nicely every time he moved. The pain seemed to be fading. Things were getting back to normal.

My passenger guided me through the streets of Monty Valley and to my father's place, where the party would take place. We soon arrived in a residential area filled with cookie-cutter houses. All were white ranches with perfectly manicured front yards. I parked my Comet and turned off the radio, which was playing a song by The Doors. My passenger got out of the car. We walked to the patio covered by a wooden pergola. An old lantern was casting a dim light, and I knocked on the door. Some of the guests had already arrived. I could hear muffled voices inside. Ash and I looked at each other while we waited.

We were smiling at each other like a couple of kids on Christmas Eve. I had been waiting for this moment since Jerry mentioned it the day before. I would finally take part in a family event and get to know the other members of the club I hadn't seen yet. Furthermore, it would be an excellent opportunity to get closer to my father, his wife, and my brother.

Finally, Casey opened the door. He and Ash exchanged a high-five, and I kissed him on the cheek. We walked through a corridor filled with family photos, and my brother showed me to the living room, which was on my right. I was right. We were the last ones to arrive. I made sure not to forget to greet every one of them with my bomb-making patient on my heels. Mona had a dazzling smile on her face, and I apologized for not having brought a gift.

"I'll make it up to you later," I said.

The warmth emanating from her reassured me.

"Having you here is already a gift, Sweetheart."

"Happy birthday," I whispered.

She kissed me. Jerry came out of the kitchen with several bottles of champagne. He opened them and served everyone. The room was pleasantly crowded. The cream color and simple décor gave a welcoming feel to the place. I was surprised by my father and Mona's classic taste, as their fashion choices were completely different. With skinny ripped jeans, Mona was displaying her rock-n-roll style, even if there was no sign of it in the interior of her home. She was also wearing a transparent black shirt over a bustier. I had to admit I wouldn't have dared to wear that outfit, even at my age. I had no body image issues, but I was self-conscious. Maybe things would change when I got older.

Everyone cheered happily, and we tried to find a spot to sit on the couches. Some sat on the armrests, and others stood. I got acquainted with Billy's wife. Her name was Rebecca, or Beckie, as most of the guys called her. She must have been in her fifties, and her style was rather conservative. She couldn't have been more different from her husband. She was easy to talk to, and we realized we had a lot in common. She was a kindergarten teacher at the local school. I had always admired people who were able to patiently manage a class full of young kids. It wasn't for me.

I also learned about Mrs. Bigma, or I should say Mrs.

Marcus Flint. Louisa was her first name. Her hair was styled in a perfect retro hairdo dating from the Roaring Twenties. I found her gorgeous and extremely elegant. They were the only couple with kids at the party. Were they the only ones to have young children? That was plausible. The twins, Samsara and Ottis, spent their time running around the house, screaming. I wasn't familiar enough with kids to estimate precisely how old they were. But I was charmed by the little girl with her braids full of colored beads. After drinking a few bottles of beer, my father started his speech. A respectful silence fell over the room.

"Thanks for coming. It means a lot to me that you've all come to celebrate my beautiful wife."

"You are such a secretive man!" Mona told him, winking at him. "All of you are. Thank you so much."

Jerry nodded, an amused smile on his face. "As you know, I am not a great cook. So, I asked Pacho for help. I invited him to celebrate with us, but he had other plans. Still, he had time to make his famous chili. So, let's dig in! Enjoy, my friends! These are precious moments."

Everyone toasted with the president of the Wild Crows, and I watched, fascinated. His natural leadership captivated me. His magnetism was so intense that any politician would envy him. I felt proud, proud to be his daughter and proud to be part of his life. He and Mona presided over the table, side by side. The kids ate in front of the TV in the living room. That was the only solution to fit everybody in.

A gigantic bowl of chili with a delicious spicy smell waited for us. I let everyone sit first, as I had no clue where I should go, and I took the last chair available. I was facing my brother, and I had Ash on my right and Mack on my left. The evening would be exciting. Mona thanked us all for coming once more, and we started to eat. It was so tasty. I knew damn well Pacho deserved the nickname of " the god of enchiladas" I had given him, but it went further than that! He was a fantastic cook. Everyone was in a party mood, and laughter filled the room. Mack glanced at me several times, and I enjoyed ignoring him. It would teach him a lesson. When his foot accidentally touched mine, I stepped on it. He grumbled so loud that everyone stopped talking.

"I burnt myself," he mumbled, lifting a glass of water. "It's delicious but damn hot!"

I repressed a laugh. The guy was quick on the draw. He knew how to turn a situation around. I kept on eating as if nothing happened, and he stopped hitting on me. That was settled. Casey entertained everyone with the story of the day his parents met. They all knew the tale, but half of the assembly laughed out loud. I also discovered some of my father's hidden talents, like singing love songs after drinking several bottles of whisky or how he stole the pretty young woman from a guy stupid enough not to see how lucky he was to have her by his side.

He did all he could to steal Mona's heart, and their mutual love for this peculiar lifestyle created a tight bond between them. Embarrassing memories followed, encouraged by the fruity notes of a good bottle of red wine. What would be a family gathering without its shameful little secrets being told? We laughed a lot. Hanger told us about the time Marcus, alias Bigma, proposed to Louisa, leading a procession of Harleys, which ended up in the schoolyard where she worked. I saw the big man under a different light.

His imposing physical appearance gave the false impression he was cold. The dark-skinned giant was intimidating, but on that night, he was approachable. It was true for every man around the table. What seemed frightening when I arrived felt more intimate. I could feel shared happiness in the air. Things were changing. I was changing. The more I hung out with them, the more I discovered a new side of me. It had always been there, but it was hidden deep inside, waiting for an emotional trigger to resurface, and the trigger had been my father.

Then, it was Hanger's turn to confide in us. He told us about a time when he and Ash escaped an army of mad dogs. He didn't give the reason why they were being chased, but he explained how they survived. According to Hanger, the secret was the powerful bestial roar they had let out to scare them. The dogs had turned around with their tails between their legs, but Ash added an essential detail to the story. A shot had been fired through the air.

Everyone laughed heartily, and I listened, fascinated by all their unbelievable stories. My peaceful life seemed so dull! I noticed their jokes were less salty than usual. It was probably because of their spouses. I suddenly realized that I was now part of their family. Having me around felt natural to them. They didn't make any special effort. They acted naturally around me.

I felt even more integrated than Billy or Marcus'

wives, even though the guys had known them for years. They didn't live within the club. They had to accept its rules because it was part of their husbands' lives. For me, things were different. I was the president's daughter. It had been my choice to join them. I had freely entered this world where I wanted to belong. I looked around the table, and all I could see was love. More than a family, it was a tightly knit and indestructible clan.

We ended the meal with strawberry shortcake and champagne. I really hoped I wouldn't cross paths with the sheriff or his deputy on my way home. I didn't feel drunk, but I was sure the police would disagree. Jerry surprised me again. He played some music to keep the party going. Marcus and Louisa excused themselves since the children were falling asleep on the couch. It was time for them to leave. Lazar, Billy, and Beckie soon followed them, saying they were too old to stay up that late. My father and his companions laughed at the eldest member of the club. According to them, the older couple could stay awake whenever they had a strong motivation to do so. Foxy left soon after. Mack and Gale went out to get some fresh air. I found their bond amusing.

The house was filled with happiness, and the presidential couple danced lovingly to the emblematic melody of *Crimson and Clover*. I watched them, moved by their smiles. I cleared the table while the hostess was cuddling up with her husband, and Casey helped me, smoking weed. I felt teleported to the seventies for a moment.

"Great party," I told my brother as I put away some plates in the dishwasher.

"They always are, you know," he said after thinking for

a few seconds. "Things are not always simple at the club. We have to enjoy these little moments."

I totally understood what he was trying to say, and I smiled at him sweetly. I spontaneously put my arm around his shoulders and then walked back to the living room. Jerry dipped Mona back while she held on to him, letting out a contagious laugh. Then they resumed their dance as if the world around them didn't exist.

I walked to Ash and put a hand on his shoulder. "Can I give you a ride home, Mister T?"

It was a reference to his real name, but it also reminded me of the master of explosives, the famous barracuda from the A-Team. He snapped out of his contemplative state and raised an eyebrow. He grumbled as he was getting up. His legs were probably stiff.

"What did you say?" Ash asked. "No, not you!"

"Dunno. Nicknames are rather fun, after all."

"No, no, no," he said, moving his finger under my nose. "Giving nicknames, that's my thing."

"All of you play this game," I corrected him. "But I must admit you're the best at it. Even though Mack is not bad himself..."

As I was speaking of the devil, he appeared. The ex-con still took a minute to applaud Mona and Jerry's performance on the way.

"You are still talking about me!" the handsome blond guy teased me.

I gave him a forced smile.

"If you like to think so." Then I turned to Ash. "Shall we go?"

Laughing, he nodded his head, and we said goodbye to

my brother, who had gone back to the improvised dance floor to play air guitar to Creedence Clearwater Revival. I couldn't help but laugh again. I wished Gale goodnight, and when I was about to do the same with Mack, he discreetly whispered in my ear, pretending to kiss me on the cheek.

"You win. I give up. I won't bother you anymore. You can consider yourself lucky. I don't usually do this. It's a pity. You and me, it could have been great."

I could see a smirk in his blond beard, and I looked at him quizzically.

"I am waiting for you, Baby Girl!" Ash shouted from the front door.

"Well... Thanks," I whispered back, still shaken by his words.

I left him there and thought about my stupid reaction as I was walking back to my father. *Thanks.* Did I really say that? In my defense, how was I supposed to react to his confession? I gave a kiss to my dad and his wife before thanking them warmly for inviting me to this great party. I knew I would remember it for a long time.

We walked back to my Comet, and I turned on the engine, praying hard not to cross paths with a police car on the way back. That said, I was with Ash, and I knew I could count on his persuasiveness. He had been so helpful the last time. It was obviously convenient to know the members of the sheriff's team. I played back the strange scene in my mind, and a question came to my lips.

"Who is Lizbeth?" My question seemed to surprise him. I tried to explain it. "When you helped me escape the deputy's clutches, you asked him to say 'Hi' to Lizbeth. Who is she? His wife?"

"Miss Detective is back," he joked. "Not only is she his wife, but she is also my sister," he confided in me.

I turned right at the intersection and suddenly realized what it meant. "Your sister? Married to the deputy?"

The look on his face was priceless. He looked apathetic, and I laughed out loud.

"Ironic, isn't it?" he said. "I mean, for an outlaw."

I started to laugh even louder and made a quick gesture to apologize. I put my hand on his shoulder. Then, I tried to regain my composure to ensure I was driving safely.

"No kidding," I said. "I can't imagine what family gatherings are like!"

The more tired I got, the more I laughed.

"Now you know why I'd rather go to the club's parties!"

We laughed together, and I parked in front of his place. I tried to calm down before wishing him goodnight.

"If you need a ride tomorrow, call me," I said.

"Thanks."

He was sincere. I could read it in his eyes.

"You're welcome," I replied. "I know it's annoying to depend on others, but it won't last."

"Yeah. So, I won't have a nurse by my side tonight?"

"No. You are getting better by the minute. The critical period is behind us. You deserve your own special time!" I joked.

He smiled at me and opened his door. As he was about to walk away, I shouted at him, "I left everything you need to change your bandages until the end of the week. It's on the table in the living room. If you have any concerns, call me."

"Yes, Mom."

"I'll check it next week."

"Alright, Mom," he repeated.

"Get out!"

With a smirk on his face, he looked at me and then disappeared into the night. I started to drive home, my mind full of memories of shared happiness. They were simple but intense moments of joy, sealed by the word "family."

23

JOE

The days following the party passed uneventfully. I hadn't seen Ash since the party, and it was probably a good sign. I went to the Devil's Trip around 6.00 p.m., and I spent my time watching the entrance door, expecting customers to walk through. The evening was dull. Maybe it was better this way, as Mona was off, and I had feared being swamped with customers. Nothing like that happened.

Most of the guys didn't show up, and it felt strange not to see them all seated around the bar. It was too quiet or not lively enough, depending on how you saw things. Only Gale, Jerry, Hanger, and Mack kept me company. It was not a full house. Luckily, I was the kind of girl to see the glass half full rather than half empty. When I finished serving a table of women, which was somewhat rare in this place, my father called to me. Puzzled, I started to walk back to the small group of bikers.

"Sweetie, could you do me a favor?" he asked.

"Yeah, of course," I answered without even thinking twice.

"I need to go back home. Could you close the bar tonight?"

"Of course," I reassured him.

"Perfect. Gale and Mack will stay with you. They'll make sure you're safe."

I looked at them, and they nodded.

"Okay."

I smiled and served beers to my so-called bodyguards. Jerry gave them his instructions and kissed me on the forehead. I was watching him walk away when Gale caught up with him.

"Wait, we need to talk about the transfer," Gale told Jerry.

My father gave me a furtive look, then turned his back to me. The music was loud enough for them to speak without being overheard. Nevertheless, I was too close. Even though they tried to be discreet, I heard most of their conversation while I was changing the keg.

"It's for the day after tomorrow, in the evening. Hang, and Mack will come with me," said the strong blond guy.

"Fine. In this case, fewer men are better. We want to keep a low profile. And it's a definite no. Mack is not coming."

"Jerry, he's had his problems, but that's water under the bridge," intervened Gale. "He's changed. And you know he's my partner."

"Yeah, I know. But it's too sensitive."

My father put his hand on Gale's strong shoulder. I pretended to be busy, but I made sure I was close enough to hear everything I could about their business, even though I knew I was playing with fire.

"I'm not kidding, Gale. I'm warning you."

Jerry's voice was harsh. I was stunned. What were they talking about? What were they supposed to transfer? Where to? Why would Mack be such a threat that my father felt it was necessary to threaten Gale?

A rapid glance in their direction told me that they agreed, despite the annoyed look I could see on my father's face.

"You're the boss," Gale said. "In three days, our debt will be history."

"Yeah, and I'm counting on you to do a clean job. We have enough on our plate right now."

"You can trust me, Boss."

My father patted Gale's jaw in a grandfatherly way.

Mack chose that moment to call me at the counter. "Joe! Do you need any help back there?"

It dawned on me that he hadn't called me by one of his silly nicknames. Furthermore, he was offering his help, without asking anything in return. What was the catch?

"Yes, please," I answered, a bit surprised.

The handsome blond guy with a strange hairstyle walked behind the bar and removed the empty keg. He put it away in the back room without asking for instructions. When he came back, he was rolling a brand new one over the hardwood floor and then put it in place. He didn't even hit on me or say a stupid joke. I couldn't believe it. I thanked him again and noticed that my father had left. In the meantime, Gale was back on his stool, followed by Mack. Hanger was getting aroused by Carla, a sweetie who was not a regular.

"So, the two of you have been friends for a long time, haven't you?" I asked the two blond guys.

Gale answered first, as Mack was busy checking out the gorgeous brunette, who was trying to seduce Hanger.

"You can say that!"

Chatting with his partner brought Mack back to reality, making him forget about his erotic fantasies.

"It always has been us against the world!" they said in unison before sipping their beer.

"You and I have been pretty wild boys, right?" Mack said.

I was right. Those two were joined at the hip.

"Anyway," declared Hanger after a few minutes, "if you don't mind, I'm out of here. Jerry didn't say I had to stay to help you close the bar!"

He grinned, and Gale punched his shoulder. The big guy put on his leather jacket and left after kissing Carla on the cheek. Walking confidently, he left, waving his hand.

As time went on, the bar cleared. At eleven sharp, it was time for me to wrap things up. I quickly wiped the tables I had just cleared and saw Carla on Mack's knees. They were engaged in a long and passionate French kiss. As I watched them running their hands shamelessly over each other's intimate parts, I realized I was right about the hot, wild boy. When I went back to the register to count the evening's proceeds, Gale raised an eyebrow and laughed, as he was watching me.

"You'll get used to it," he joked before finishing his beer.

"Used to what?"

"To this," he said, pointing at the amorous couple as Carla was now sitting astride Mack. "A true Don Juan! Women want him!"

"Oh, you mean this! Yeah, that's what I've heard."

I ignored the show. At least I had no regrets turning him down several times. To him, I had only been another challenge. The novelty was wearing off, and I was no longer at the top of his long list. I was at peace with it. I cleared their glasses after locking the register. Then, I quickly cleaned the wooden counter.

"We are closing," I told the sweetie so she would interrupt her kissing.

I was surprised by their stamina. Neither had come for air in a while. Moaning reluctantly, she let Mack go, giving him a look full of promises, and then she stood up. If I hadn't been so tired, I might have been embarrassed.

"Are you coming?" she complained.

"Go to my bike and wait for me. I'll only be a minute."

Without a second look, he let her leave. I told the guys they could go home and turned off the lights before locking the bar behind us. I thanked them, and Gale walked to his Harley, which was parked a little further along. Mack, on the other hand, didn't move a muscle. Looking sort of like James Dean, he lit up a cigarette. I looked at him, wondering what his intentions might be.

"You can go, Mack."

He took a puff and then blew out the smoke as he laughed silently. Two dimples appeared in his blond beard, but I quickly turned my eyes away from this sweet picture.

"I follow orders. Your father asked us to stay with you. He's concerned about your safety. So, until you get to this apartment of yours, I'm staying with you."

He was displaying the smile of an irresistible bad boy. A little devil looking like an angel.

"I'm going home. I live three floors to climb. You can go. I think Carla is waiting for you."

He smiled again. His blue eyes were sparkling.

"Don't tell me you're jealous!" he said.

The man had guts!

"Not at all!"

"Fine. You really made me believe you were, for a moment! And I would have been pissed! Especially after turning me down so many times..."

His lack of manners made me laugh in spite of myself.

"You're wrong. You can date whoever you want. I don't care, Mack."

"I'm relieved," he teased me. "This is how we roll around here."

"What are you talking about?"

He crushed his cigarette butt on the ground and seemed thoughtful as he blew out smoke.

"You're just discovering the outlines of our world. To be honest, we have a bad habit of getting into trouble. Fate makes us pay by playing tricks on us. We don't complain about it. We chose this life, nobody forced us. We get used to it. When something good comes into our world, and everything runs rather smoothly, we enjoy it because we know it's not going to last. Sooner or later, shit always happens."

I was speechless, stunned to see Mack looking so serious. I had only seen him with his mask of arrogance. In his eyes, I could read a tumult of emotions, a certain nostalgia and resignation. I couldn't even remember how our conversation had started. I just knew it was trivial, so I wondered how we came to switch to such a grave and serious exchange of words.

"Why are you telling me all this?" I asked.

He smiled again, but this time, his smile was simple and straightforward. Mack was standing in front of me, looking sincere. I looked over his shoulder. Gale had left, but the pretty brunette, dressed in mini-shorts, was still waiting for the handsome biker to take her some place else, and apparently, she was getting impatient.

"I'm telling you this because I know you find our appetite for partying, violence, sex, and alcohol gross. We live outrageously and without limits."

"I don't get it..."

Mack took another step towards me until he was a little bit too close for comfort. Still, I didn't back down and stood straight.

"We learn how to make the most of every minute and live several lives at once, as ours will probably be short and full of uncertainty. You can't fight on the devil's side without paying the price. Why should we bother living by the rules of a society we chose to run away from? Good behavior and these so-called good manners suffocate us because we aren't afraid to be judged by others. It's bullshit! It's not for us. We are outlaws, Joe. That's about as blunt as I can get."

The word startled me. I finally had the answers to all the damn questions that had been running through my mind for the last few days. He had just awakened a part of me that I never knew was there, a dark side I had to explore. But it was alive, hidden deep inside, until that moment. Its darkness was running through my veins. I could sense it with every beat of my heart. I was one of them. I was undeniably Jerry Welsh's child. I belonged to their world. My criminal record was nothing like the Wild Crows. I wasn't a rebel, but they were extending a hand I was about to grab. The wild wind blowing on Monty Valley was intoxicating, and its calling was irresistible. It was now crystal clear. My need to lead a new and different life was engraved in my soul. I had found my place.

Before I could open my mouth, he gave me a kiss on the forehead. "Think about it, Joe. You are one of us now. Stop worrying about bullshit and enjoy life while you can."

He paused, looking a bit more like his old self.

"Go home," I said. "You're making me run late."

His mischievous expression didn't help me fight the storm of emotions that was raging inside of me. I locked my eyes on him for a few more seconds, maybe so he would tell me more. He had talked so passionately, with such an appetite for life, that I felt helpless and humbled. I nodded and then walked away. When I reached my door, I heard a loud whistle. It came from Mack, who was sitting on his bike with the pretty brunette behind him.

"Learn your lesson. Time is not on our side, Joe!" he told me in a more cheerful tone.

The engine roared, and I watched them disappear into the dark night. I stood there for a moment, ignoring the cold breeze. Then I went home and double-locked the door behind me. I had planned a fantastic date with my pillow, but I postponed it, as Mack's words had troubled me more than I thought.

I took out a beer from the fridge and found a spot to sit on my couch. I went through the list of contacts on my mobile phone and stopped when I saw Saddie's name. I hesitated for a second, aware I had forgotten to call her back. What would I tell her? Would I confess to her that my father was an outlaw dealing arms, and that I had performed surgery on a pool table? She would probably panic and call the police or even come to bring me back home herself. No, she wouldn't understand. Nobody would.

One needed to be part of this world to see the truth. If one tried to reformulate facts to make them understandable to ordinary people, their essence was modified and eventually lost. The idea that nothing could be placed above the very notion of freedom would be erased. I dropped the idea of calling her and turned the TV on. I zapped through the channels and finally settled for old music videos. A smile came to my lips, and I mechanically typed a text message on my phone.

Me: Miss Detective wants to make sure Mister-T isn't agonizing alone at home...

Going over my text message, I found it amusing, and I sent it to Ash when I was done. I drank a sip of my fresh beer and laid down on my couch, watching Bob Dylan *playing Mr. Tambourine Man.* I was startled when my phone vibrated on my chest. I had fallen asleep without realizing it.

Ash: A patient without his nurse, it sucks. Who knows what will become of me, Mini doc! Time will tell!

Still drowsy, I laughed, feeling moved by the old fool. I put my phone back down on the table along with my half-full bottle of beer. I didn't even bother going back to my bed. Lying on the couch felt good, and I let the sweet melodies of an era I wished I had known rock me back to sleep.

24

JERRY

Mona and Joe had been back for several hours. I had turned off the lights in the entire bar except for the one above my head. No matter how much I tried to settle my nerves, nothing worked. It was already two-thirty. Gale should have already called. Fuck!

I looked at my hands on the wooden counter. They bore marks, and the stress was so intense that they were shaking. It was always like this, and it would not change. There was always the anxiety of making a mistake or being struck by an unexpected event, something that would push one of my guys to make a tragic mistake.

Twelve years of presiding over this club had not made me immune to the fear of losing one of my guys. I would never get used to it. When death came knocking, we bowed our heads. Each time, we had to let it take a piece of us before moving on. Life continued, and so did we, but every loss left its mark—a new cross to carry over our worn and weathered backs.

Finally, two headlights lit the parking lot. I froze, torn between anxiety and haste. Silhouettes left the black van, and I could breathe again. I opened the door and let them in, but I almost lost my temper when I found out Mack was one of them. I patted their shoulders in the way I always did to bring us luck. Their faces were tense, and I let them sit down before asking them to give me details. They had dirt on their faces and on their clothes, too. Making himself at home, Hanger went behind the bar and took out four beers.

My attention was focused on Gale. He knew what I expected of him and how important it was to get the job done satisfactorily. That night, he had broken the first rule of this club, the respect he owed to his hierarchy. He had ignored my instructions.

"Everything is okay," he replied without any further explanation.

What an idiot! I made a real effort not to lose my temper in Mack's presence. But I would definitely discuss the matter with the man who had deliberately defied my authority.

"Damn, you could have sent a message. I was worried," I reprimanded him.

"Sorry, Boss. We came back as soon as we could. We're dead tired. Besides, we had quite a scare," said Hanger.

Puzzled, I frowned. Mack explained.

"We hit a sobriety checkpoint. Got real tense for a minute."

They watched each other before bursting into laughter. I was getting impatient and signaled them to keep on talking.

"We were so lucky, Jerry," Mack added. "The car's trunk in front of us was filled with marijuana!"

Stunned, I listened to the story, and then I burst out laughing. I couldn't believe our luck. For once, things had gone our way! All of us cheered to that, and I watched them enjoy the well-deserved reward after a tough evening.

"Unbelievable..." I said.

"Yeah," they all answered in unison.

They were still laughing. I couldn't believe how lucky they had been.

"So, all's good. Can you imagine? The van was loaded with eighty pounds of drugs!" Gale said enthusiastically.

"It was insane," Hanger whispered.

"I thought you were going to shit in your pants!" Mack provoked him.

The words were like a slap in the face.

"So, where did you store the shit?" I asked, still worried about the risks.

"Look at our faces, Boss! We did a good job," Hanger said. "We buried everything in Lestwood Forest, ten miles south of Richmond. We marked the trees with a knife."

"I'll make a phone call to the Karson Penitentiary Center tomorrow morning," Gale said.

I approved silently.

"Perfect! That's done. We won't touch this shit anymore."

I looked for approval in their eyes, and I immediately

found it. We agreed, and it reassured me. We finished our beers and put the glassware in the dishwasher. Joe or Mona would run it in the morning.

"Come on. Go home, guys. You deserve to rest, now."

No one protested. I turned off the one light left in the Devil's, and we left. I let Hanger and Mack walk to their bikes first so I could have a word with the chief of operations.

"Gale, one minute, please."

He didn't seem surprised. The tall, military-looking man stopped in his tracks and faced me. We remained silent for a few moments, waiting for the other two guys to leave. I had no doubt he understood where I was coming from. His face turned more serious. Was he worried? According to them, everything went perfectly. But in my opinion, we still had things to discuss, and I wouldn't back down, especially when it concerned such a sensitive topic.

"So, are you proud of yourself?" I asked.

I was satisfied when I noticed my words had touched him. He briefly looked away before confronting me.

"Jerry, he and I had already talked about it, even before you spoke to me. What did you want me to tell him? Sorry, but we still don't trust you?"

"It would kill me to see him relapse!" I said impatiently.

Gale looked annoyed, and I glared at him. He let out a big breath.

"I know, Boss! But he's been clean for years now. There's no reason for things to change."

"There's one, and it's handling drugs..."

"There was absolutely no risk, believe me. Mack was

on the lookout while Hanger and I took care of loading everything in the van. When we drove off, he was riding in front of us. He never touched the drugs. I made sure of it, Jerry. I promise you."

"He also knows right where to find eighty kilos. You know how that shit gets to people. It's so fucking addictive, Gale."

"I know!"

"So why did you ask him to come?"

"Because he's my friend, my brother. I couldn't imagine leaving him behind. We roll that way, you know. If he gets into trouble one day, I'll be the first one to help him. And he insisted on coming with me tonight."

"What the fuck, Gale! All I'm saying is that if you care so much about him, you shouldn't have let him get near a truck loaded with drugs!"

The atmosphere became even more electric. Both of us were annoyed. I sighed and kicked a pop can at my feet.

"Everything went smoothly, so you don't need to worry," Gale whispered.

I stared at him, and he looked away. He was perfectly aware that he was about to cross the line.

"You seem confident. I hope you're right, Gale. Really." I groaned and gave him a violent push. "You defied my authority, Gale! You disobeyed me! You had instructions, and you chose to ignore them. When you joined the club, you accepted its rules, my brother. Pull yourself together!! You need to follow the rules or leave!"

This idiot didn't have the slightest idea about the mess that his brother's fallout had created four years ago. He was not there when we had to help Mack get clean. Gale was rotting in jail. How could he even imagine what Mack had gone through for all these months? It was simply impossible. No one could understand without having experienced those moments of total darkness.

I had to remind Gale that there was a hierarchy to respect. In Karson, he had been on his own until the Black Wolves offered him protection. Within our group, he had to readapt quickly. In other words, I was keeping an eye on him. I wanted to see how things would turn out, and it would mainly depend on him. The tension in the air slowly cleared off, and we silently looked at each other for a long time. I tapped his shoulder and kept my eyes on him.

"If everything goes well, then we are cool," I said with a meaningful smile. "But get your shit together, Gale."

He nodded, but his face was still tense.

"Come on, go home! It's been a hard day."

He seemed exhausted and shaken by our conversation. A good night's sleep would probably help him think things through. I couldn't trust an ex-junkie to take care of a job involving kilos of cocaine. It would be careless and stupid. Gale was clearly minimizing what Mack had gone through, and Mack was too proud to talk about it, or too arrogant to consider that it would be hazardous for him to be involved in such an expedition. I admired him for accepting the challenge without a second thought. But experience had taught me better than to trust a former drug addict with the object of his addiction.

A guy like Mack, who had overcome his addiction, was not totally cured. The source of his problems had only disappeared momentarily. Confronted by his demons, the old temptations would resurface. I would have to keep an eye on him. Even though Gale was convinced that everything had gone well, my instincts told me to stay alert. I let him go away with a feeling of unfinished business. I put on my helmet, lit a cigarette, and then got on my old Harley Davidson.

I drove slowly to my house, enjoying the cool autumnal wind on my scruffy cheeks. The roaring of my Dyna Street Bob cheered me up. It sounded like an old song I would never get tired of.

25

JOE

People often complain about life's unpredictability, but sometimes, it works in our favor. That day, I wasn't shocked to get a call from an unknown number. Adam Jefferson clearly didn't realize that politeness was the only reason I had agreed to go out with him in the first place. Honestly, I had forgotten about him and hoped he had forgotten about me too. We had dated on and off a long time ago, but after I ended things, I rejected every attempt he made to see me again.

I had naively imagined that he had gotten the message loud and clear. Obviously, I was wrong. He had asked me to lunch, knowing that I was working evenings. I had stupidly let that information slip out when we met at the hospital. As I wasn't expecting his call, I had no time to come up with an excuse. I had to admit having lunch with him was no big deal compared to the help he gave me when Ash was shot. He had involuntarily taken risks for the club, and we owed him one. I owed him one.

All I could do was swallow my pride and accept to meet him with a forced smile–I always knew if people smiled while talking on the phone. Usually, the tone of their voice was different. But fate had other plans for me. As I turned on the engine of my Comet to make the drive to San Francisco, I heard a strange noise coming from under the hood. I froze. Then, I heard the same sound, followed by silence.

"Come on…"

An unpleasant odor of gasoline filled the car. I immediately understood what had just happened. Somewhere above me, a god I didn't really believe in had saved me from a boring date with a boring guy. I felt grateful. I thanked this higher power and then focused on the problem at hand - my car! After one last try, I realized I was making things worse. No sound came out. Now, I was starting to panic. I looked around the garage and saw Mack and Bigma smoking cigarettes in their overalls. I hurried over to them.

"Hi, Joe," Mack said, smiling.

"Hi, guys," I said hastily. "I have a problem with my car. It won't start. Can you check it out?"

Marcus joined the two men and nodded. I handed him the keys, and he took my place in the passenger seat. I noticed dark shadows below his magnificent eyes. The previous night had probably been difficult. It was not really surprising with a ladies' man like him! When he tried to start my antique car, no sound came out. The guys opened the hood, and Bigma leaned over, examining the engine expertly. He poked around and looked at a lot of things I did not know about. I watched him anxiously, hoping I wouldn't have to say my farewells to my beloved antiquity.

"It seems you've flooded the engine."

"I didn't do anything at all..."

"Yes, you did," said Marcus as he got out of the car.

"I tell you, I didn't..."

"You tried to start it at all costs. That's what flooded the engine."

"Maybe... but it didn't start, so there is a problem," I said.

"How many miles?" Marcus asked while he was still examining the engine.

"A little over a hundred thousand," I replied.

"That's reasonable considering its age."

Marcus wiped his hands and smiled at me.

"We'll have a look at it. It's pretty quiet this morning."

"Thank you! That would be great!"

"First, I need to replace the tires of the BMW that's on the bridge. I'll take care of your little bijou just after. Mack, can you start working on it?"

The blond guy jumped as if he had been lost in his thoughts. "Can't. Sorry."

His answer surprised me.

"Are you all right, Mack?" Marcus inquired.

"Yeah, it's just that I don't have time this morning. I need to be out of here in ten minutes. In fact, I'm already late."

"Late for what?" The big dark-skinned man marveled.

He looked briefly at his watch and seemed surprised.

"I told Jerry. I've just forgotten to tell you about it. I have a doctor's appointment in town. That was the only available slot he had."

"Okay. Are you sick?"

"Nothing serious," he reassured us, waving his hand. "I told you, I'm already late."

He kissed me on the cheek and walked away before I had time to say anything. I stared at Marcus for a moment. His eyes followed Mack until he reached his bike in the parking lot. Then he smiled sweetly.

"I'll take care of it in half an hour. That work for you?"

"Perfect! Do you think it's anything serious?"

He sighed and examined the Comet again. A smirk appeared on his full lips. "I'll have to take a closer look, but there is a good chance it's nothing serious. I guess the carburetor is a little dirty, nothing else."

It reassured me a little. I wouldn't have to say my good-byes to my beloved car anytime soon. I was hopeful. I would get it back. On the other hand, I wouldn't be able to see Adam Jefferson soon. I felt almost happy. I had to admit I was relieved not to have to listen to his advice about a healthy and balanced life or the long list of his accomplishments for an hour or two. I dialed his number, which I had added to my phone earlier in the morning, and told him my car had broken down. I played my part, trying to sound disappointed.

He offered to pick me up, but I refused to suppress a little laugh. The good doctor meeting the guys at the work-shop would have been like letting loose an innocent little chicken in a barn filled with hungry foxes. I pretended to be concerned about my car and told him that I wanted to stay around to make sure everything would turn out fine. He sounded disappointed. I had just ruined his plans once again. This time, I apologized more sincerely, conscious that canceling a date at the last moment wasn't a nice thing to do. In my defense, I was anxious about my car, but this twist of events was the perfect reason to escape Adam and his well-rehearsed seduction speech. I told him we would see each other sometime soon, adding I would get back to him, which was probably the best way to avoid being called the next day. Then I hung up.

I waited in the workshop and watched Marcus as he was driving a silver BMW down the ramp.

"Are you working alone here?"

"Today, yes. Well, Mack was supposed to be with me. We have a shift work schedule."

"Oh, I see."

"Sometimes, we just hang out outside or take care of our own bikes."

I nodded and looked at the very place where I had met my first Wild Crow member, aka Lazarus. I was frightened then. He was so big, so strong, so... tattooed! Bigma finished tightening the tires, then he parked the vehicle in the outside parking lot. A few minutes later, he went to my Comet, pulling along a rolling tool carriage. I followed him like a lost dog. To be honest, I knew nothing about mechanics. Although I was delighted to own an antique car, I had no clue how it worked. Marcus dived under the hood, and all I could do was watch his expert gestures.

"It looks complicated," I said.

"Not if you take a little interest. Mechanics are pretty predictable."

"Predictable," I said pensively. "That's great. It's something rare."

"Yeah?"

We laughed together before he turned his attention back to the mysterious metallic tubes.

"I'd like to learn one day. I mean, the basics. I'd like to be able to fix it when there's a small problem."

Marcus looked at me with a raised eyebrow and laughed.

"What?" I asked, a bit upset.

"Nothing! Don't get me wrong, but you don't seem to be the kind of girl who could listen to an engine."

I probably looked bewildered.

"You're wrong, Marcus. I could surprise you!"

The giant burst out laughing, and his joyful mood was contagious. Suddenly, I heard two engines getting closer, and there were no customers. That unmistakable metallic rumble could only mean two powerful bikes ruling the road.

On the first one, I recognized my father despite his dark sunglasses. He had a peculiar jaw, and few men smiled like this when they saw me. Behind him was a man I did not expect to see anytime soon, or at least not on his own bike. They parked close to us and took off their helmets and glasses, finally revealing their faces.

My dad took me in his arms and greeted Bigma with a slap on the back as his hands were buried in my carburetor. Ash winced slightly as he got off his motorcycle, probably because of his injury. I had not seen him for ten days, and I assumed he was recovering at home. He greeted us with a smile, then joined Marcus to look under the open hood of my Mercury Comet.

"Is there a problem?"

"The carburetor is dirty," Marcus answered without shifting his attention. "The girl could not start it."

"Do you need a hand?"

"Nope, I'm almost done. I would have parked it some-place else before starting to work on it, but Mack went to the doctor's office, so..."

"Mack is where?" my father asked.

There was a long silence. Bigma and I looked at each other.

"Yeah, he said he told you. He had to leave early this morning..."

"Not that I know of!" my father said in a stunned voice.

Something was wrong, and I felt I was getting involved in something that didn't concern me. Maybe lunch with Adam might not have been such a bad idea...

"What did he tell you exactly?"

What I heard in my father's voice wasn't surprise but suspicion—or something like it. The wrinkles on his fore-head grew deeper. Why did he seem so concerned that Mack had left work without saying anything? Bigma understood it was serious because he put down his tools and interrupted his open-heart surgery on my Comet.

"He just said that he had an appointment with his doctor and that he had told you about it. Nothing else. Why?"

It was confusing seeing my father think over every word

as if they had a secret hidden meaning. Something was off, but I couldn't figure out what it was. Apparently, I was not one of those geniuses who could decipher encrypted sentences.

"Is there a problem, Jerry?"

Ash moved closer to us. He was visibly worried too.

"I don't know," Jerry answered under his breath. "Let's see what happens next."

His words were barely audible. The next second, he was walking away with his phone stuck to his ear. He disappeared into the Devil's Trip. His pace was slow, and he was clearly preoccupied. Marcus looked at me before resuming his work on my Comet. Ash frowned intently, and I noticed the anxiety on his face. With a nod, I invited him to follow me. He got the message. I felt luck was on my side. We walked to the parking lot, and I tried to lighten the atmosphere.

"You were supposed to call me so I could check your wound at the beginning of the week."

"Yeah," whispered Ash in a distant voice. "I forgot. Sorry, Mini Doc."

He seemed preoccupied like Jerry. He kept looking in the direction of the bar. What was going on with Mack was a mystery to me, but they seemed to know something I didn't. Did it have anything to do with the conversation I overheard between my father and Gale a few days ago? I had no clue, but I suspected that no one would tell me.

First, the club's business was something to be discussed between its members at the table, not with women. Secondly, no one would talk about this with the boss's daughter for obvious safety reasons. So, I dropped the matter. Ash sat on a rusted cooler, and I tried to ignore his distant attitude.

"Can you show me?" I asked/

He didn't seem to understand, so I explained.

"I'm talking about your wound."

"Oh, yeah."

The tall, dark-haired man lifted his jacket and his shirt so I could check his scar.

"No bandage?"

"It only put one when I think about it."

I sighed and knelt to observe it. I was satisfied with the job I had done, especially considering the difficult conditions.

"No infection. It's healing well."

"Yeah, I told you. I would have called you if I had a problem."

"I am sure of it," I joked, giving him an amused look.

To be perfectly honest, I very much doubted that he would have called me for help unless he was about to die or could no longer move. He was too proud. I let him pull his clothes down and watched him pensively. I was so curious I couldn't resist and tried my luck.

"Ash, what's the matter with Mack?"

He stared at me for a moment, then shook his head, scowling. The usually cheerful man froze.

"There's nothing to say. It does not concern you, Joe. Sorry."

"I overheard a discussion between my father and Gale. I was wondering... Maybe you could tell me more."

He stepped toward me, leaving me speechless. The darkness in his eyes was so intense that I couldn't tell if he was the same guy I'd laughed with just last week while watching hippie music videos. He looked like a different person.

Ash nervously ran a hand over his beard. "You ask too many questions, Joe. You know it's wrong. I'm your father's right-hand man and his best friend. Don't use me to get the info that he would not give you himself. If you want to know something, go directly to him. You cannot interfere with the club. What happens in the Wild Crows, stays in the Wild Crows, Gorgeous."

I was stunned. His gaze was terrifying. In his words, I could hear a warning, which surprised me. Furthermore, his attitude towards me had been so cold that I did not know how to behave. I acted like a scolded kid would.

"Okay..."

Ash nodded. As he was about to leave, I thought of something important. "I was there when he left this morning."

I had caught his attention. Puzzled, he turned to face me.

"I was there, and he seemed very tired. He looked like someone who had not slept for a long time. After all, it's Mack... I guess he's a night owl..."

Ash seemed captivated by my revelations. He came even closer to me, his eyes locked on mine.

"I don't know what's going on with him. Maybe he's sick, or he has a problem... Anyway, I want to help." I paused, remembering Mack's face before he left. "He looked terrible. Bigma asked him to start working on my car while he was finishing up the BMW. He turned white.

That's when he said he had to go. He seemed scared... it was weird, really. Like he had seen a ghost."

Ash sighed and let out a heartless laugh. "A ghost, huh?"

"Yes."

Once more, he ignored me and seemed lost in his thoughts. With his eyes shut, he turned his head back towards the bar.

"Thanks, Joe."

That was all I could get from him that morning, and I learned nothing more about the situation.

"I just want to help," I whispered.

But Ash had already left to join my father. I was scared. I worried that something terrible was about to happen since the two most influential members of the club seemed extremely concerned by Mack's attitude. It was the first time I could feel such tension in the air since I arrived.

26

JERRY

I asked Ash and Billy to join me for dinner that night. There was no need to gather everyone. For now, we just had suspicions. I did not pick the two guys out randomly. They were the men I felt the closest to. We were the eldest members, not necessarily in terms of age, but in terms of seniority under the banner of the Wild Crows. Only Lazar was missing, but I thought it would be better to leave him alone right then. His heart had been weak for two years now. It wouldn't have been wise to stress him out unnecessarily.

They arrived a little early, and we all took a seat. My right-hand man's face was tense. I could understand why. He knew what was going on, and he shared my doubts. On the other hand, it would be news to Billy. His round, bearded face was expressing his intense curiosity.

"I asked you to come because I need help on a confidential matter," I began, immediately captivating my two guests' attention. "It seems premature to let anyone know about this because right now, I've got no proof. And that's where you come in. I need answers. Ash already knows the topic."

I turned to Billy. With my hands joined on the wooden table, I tried to figure out the best way to bring the matter up. Billy was old school, just like me, Ash, and Lazar. He liked to get straight to the point. Small talk and other bullshit weren't welcome when we were discussing the club's affairs.

So, I just spilled out the beans, staring at the club logo engraved in the middle of the table. "I have a bad feeling about Mack."

"What do you mean?"

"I've been keeping an eye on him since he participated in the delivery for the Black Wolves with Gale and Hang. Three days ago, he sneaked out of the garage, and since then, I haven't been able to reach him. Nobody has seen him."

Instinctively, Billy winced.

"It sucks. He should not have been there."

"We agree on this one," I interjected. "Gale went too far."

"He screwed up," Ash said, looking away.

I nodded.

"I'm not sure of anything right now. I do not have the slightest proof that he is using again. But I want to get to the bottom of this and make sure he's still clean. I had the forest checked—nothing's moved, for now"

"What the fuck, Jerry..."

Billy's voice sounded like a faint, reproachful complaint. I understood. I had just revived an unpleasant memory. If my instinct was wrong, I would be the happiest man on earth. But it was rarely the case when I smelled a rat. I had a powerful sixth sense.

"I talked to your daughter on the day Mack left work," Ash said.

I stared at him, not understanding the link between Joe and the problem at hand.

"She wanted to make sure my wound was not infected," he pointed out, almost defensively.

I was usually amused when I sensed he was afraid of me, but the matter we were discussing was far too serious. If we lost Mack, we could lose the club. Drugs took no prisoners, and they were highly addictive. They alienated their victims, who became capable of the worst, including selling their father and mother for one more dose. We hadn't reached that point yet.

At least, I hoped. I knew how catastrophic and fast the fallout could be. And when it came to recovering junkies, the speed at which they self-destroyed was dramatically faster. I knew the problem only too well. Mack was the last man we'd had to save from its clutches, and it had not been a walk in the park. I didn't want to go through it again, but I would do whatever needed to be done. I had no other choice.

Mack was part of our family, despite the demon that was eating him away and would taunt him for the rest of his life. On the other hand, one thing prevailed. I wouldn't let him put the club in danger.

Therein lay the problem.

Billy seemed to fully understand my worries. He was not born yesterday. He was knowledgeable about drugs, and he knew about Mack's problem with heroin. A junkie was never entirely out of the woods.

"Joe was with Marcus when Mack left work," Ash said. "According to her, he looked awful. He seemed exhausted. She told me that when Marcus asked him to take care of the Comet, he turned as white as a ghost. He seemed to be scared, and then he left, just like that, pretending to have talked with Jerry about leaving early."

"Bullshit! He didn't say anything," I said to Billy.

He remained thoughtful for a long time. He was probably processing the information. For my part, I had spent the last two days thinking over and over. Each time, I reached the same conclusion, and it was one that scared me.

"It's not like him to lie. Not to the club, and not to you," Billy said.

He couldn't accept the truth.

"That's what worries me," I admitted painfully.

"I'll try to reach him, and I'll have a casual talk with Gale," Ash said.

"Stay discreet. I don't want to raise any red flags. Nothing good ever comes from stirring shit. Lie low until we know more."

My right-hand man nodded silently, frowning.

"Billy, I'm gonna ask you to tail him..."

"No problem."

"Take the white van parked behind the workshop. It's less noticeable than your bike."

The older man nodded.

"Who else knows about this?" he asked.

I made a quick mental inventory.

"Just us three. Marcus and Joe have suspicions, but nothing more."

I paused and turned my focus to Ash. When I met my brother's eyes, I had a last request. And I would not tolerate being turned down.

"I don't want my daughter to be involved in this mess. I know she gets along with Mack. I do not want him around her, at least not until we know what we are dealing with. I don't want to see her caught in the middle of a drug war."

"Got it," he replied.

He seemed a bit puzzled, so I explained. "She is curious, and she likes talking to you. I don't want her to know anything."

"She won't," he reassured me with an honest look.

I sighed and leaned back on my chair.

I had not used my gavel for this informal meeting. It was over, and we all went back home, looking for a little comfort. Mine was in the kitchen, and her name was Mona. When everything seemed to go the wrong way with the club, she was the rock I could hold on to so I could keep my head above the water. The club did not allow women at the table. It was a man's organization, and for historical and cultural reasons, it would not change.

There were some women who were happy to gravitate around us, help us with our business, and take care of us without asking any questions. The less they knew, the better it was... It was probably the best way to shelter them. Mona had been by my side for many stormy years, and she had never given up on me. Many would have run away! She was the only woman to possess a Wild Crows jacket.

Her daily dedication to our group, her eagerness to help us in difficult times, and the love she was giving us had won over the club, even the most macho guys. She would never be a real member, but she had earned her spot among us. When I started the mechanic workshop and bought the bar and the motel, she was not supposed to be involved.

But she had made a conscious choice to share my entire life, including its excesses and risks. We had gone through some tough times and seen some heads roll, even though a few were innocent victims. I always got back on my feet because I had her back, and she had mine.

Walking to the front door, I took off my leather jacket. It was like removing the tough guy's mask I had to wear when I was with the guys. My weaknesses, flaws, and fears resurfaced immediately, and only her smile could soothe me.

It only took her a split second to realize that something was wrong. One glance was enough for her to understand the extent of my fear and doubts. She hugged me tightly, and her embrace made me feel alive and stronger. She gave me a positive outlook for the future. When I was in her arms, I held on to those good thoughts.

27

JOE

Marcus had refused any payment for the work done on my car. Even though I had been on his back for the last three days with my wallet in hand, looking like a mad woman, all I could achieve was making him laugh. It drove me nuts. It was not my style to take advantage of people. So that morning, I tried to trick him. Since he didn't want my money, maybe he would accept a delicious breakfast. I bought different pastries at the local bakery before making a stop at the coffee shop located near the park. With a broad smile on my face, I walked into the workshop with my bag of pastries in one hand and four steaming paper cups in a cup holder in the other. I knew the guys never worked alone. Usually, they were in a group of two or three.

I was lucky! I bumped into my target. Dressed in an

orange jumpsuit like the prisoners wore behind bars, Marcus was looking at a Harley-like motorbike. Its chromed logo indicated it was a "Victory" model. It was absolutely fabulous. Its dark gray and matte paint gave an original touch to the work of art, and it bore a star similar to the ones featured on World War II vehicles.

"Nice bike," I said, trying to surprise him.

He jumped and banged his head against the toolbox behind him. I repressed a laugh and offered him the food.

"Hey, Joe," he greeted me, smiling. "Next time, don't startle me like that! My skull doesn't appreciate it."

He rubbed his head, and I apologized with a childish pout.

"I have a good reason for coming. You don't want my money, but every work deserves a fair reward."

Marcus raised an eyebrow, so I explained.

"Croissants, cupcakes, and hot coffee," I said proudly, showing him the feast I had prepared. A soft smile crossed his shaved face. I had nailed it.

"It works for me!" he said, amused. "But do not tell Louisa. She's trying to put me on a diet!"

I winked and swore not to say anything. The next thing I knew, he had already grabbed a cup of coffee in his large hands.

"Are you alone?" I asked.

Still eating, he made a negative gesture.

"Coffee!" he shouted out in a deep voice.

A metallic noise echoed in the back. It sounded like a key that had fallen on the concrete floor. Then, I heard two guys talking, and they finally appeared. Foxy and Ash walked toward us with hungry smiles.

"You're spoiling us!" the youngest said happily.

Even though he was twenty-seven, he looked like a kid, and his face covered in freckles, was angelic.

"Mini-Doc," Ash greeted me wickedly.

As the three of them grabbed pastries and a cup of coffee, I chatted a little.

"Marcus did not want to accept money for repairing my car. So, I decided to repay him differently!"

Ash choked, so Foxy slapped him brutally on the back to help him swallow. Then, they laughed out loud as Bigma half-heartedly looked at them.

"Gorgeous," he told me, "you'd better pay attention to the words you use in here. This place is full of perverts."

"Wrong," Ash mumbled, his voice still hoarse. "I'm not a pervert."

"Liar!" Bigma retorted.

"No, I like sex, it's different. I think there is no harm in having a good time, that's all!" he boasted.

"What does it have to do with my croissants?"

My detached tone unsettled him, and he looked me in the eye. I felt like I was dealing with two kids, one of whom was almost fifty years old.

"I feel sorry for you, Marcus. Working with these two must be hard."

"You bet!" replied the tall man, pretending to feel weary.

As I grabbed a croissant before they all disappeared, my phone vibrated in the back pocket of my jeans. I snatched it and realized Mack was calling. I was speechless. It was the first time he had ever contacted me by phone. I only had his number because my father had asked me to add all the members' contact info as a safety measure. And as far as I knew, no one had heard from him for days now.

Hesitantly, I put the phone to my ear and tried to speak in a confident tone. "Hi," I said.

"Hi, Joe."

There was a brief silence, then he spoke in a shaky voice. "Joe, tell me... could you pick me up, please?"

Was he drunk? I didn't understand what he meant.

"What? You mean, meet you? Where are you, Mack?"

Surprised, I spoke louder. I probably should have been more discreet. Ash, Foxy, and Marcus were close to me. I walked a few steps, but it was probably too late. They were all staring at me, apparently curious about what was going on. I heard a sigh at the end of the line. Was he tired or annoyed? It was strange. Something was definitely wrong.

"I'm at Lone Street and Main Court, right after the abandoned slaughterhouse."

Confused, I nodded. Why was he there? The place sounded shady and creepy!

"What are you doing there?" I asked.

"I... I don't know. I got drunk last night, and I woke up there... without my bike," he replied.

He was ashamed. I could hear it in his voice. I was worried about him.

"But why me?" I asked.

My question probably sounded strange, but I needed to know what I was getting into. The logical thing to do would have been to call one of the guys... so why had he phoned me? It didn't make any sense. I heard a grunt on the other side of the line.

"The guys would have picked on me..."

"Even Gale?"

"He's not answering his phone."

I took a few seconds to think it over. His distressed tone made me give in. "I'll be there in fifteen minutes."

I was about to hang up when I heard his voice. "Joe!"

"What?"

"I am sorry..."

"Don't worry about it. Don't move. I'm on my way."

"... Thank you."

I finally hung up and started to think. I had never heard Mack so distressed before. I could feel his pain over the phone. When I turned around, the guys were waiting to listen to what I had to say.

Ash got straight to the point. "Where is he?"

I was worried. I couldn't tell why he sounded so upset. Was it worry or anger? What would they do to Mack if they could get their hands on him? If he had called me, it was probably because he had something to hide from his brothers-in-arms. I felt trapped. The tall, dark-haired man stepped forward, closing in on me. I was intimidated, so I confessed. I thought I could trust him. At least, that was what I was hoping for.

"He's in town. He woke up in a deserted place, and his motorcycle was gone. I'm on my way to go and get him."

I did not wait to see their reactions and walked to my car.

Ash caught up with me. "No, you stay here. I'll take care of it."

"No way!" I protested. "If he called me, he must have had his reasons. I'm going."

His jaw hardened. Women usually didn't go against his orders. Even worse, he considered me a "kid," but I had no intention of letting Mack down, at least not until I knew more about what was going on.

"You stay here!" he said more vehemently.

"You are not the boss of me!" I replied in the same tone without looking down.

I should have been intimidated, but my pride prevailed. I was a free woman, goddamn it! My rebellious attitude made him furious, and he disappeared into the back of the workshop. Marcus and Foxy were looking at each other, apparently trying to keep a low profile. I quickly walked towards my Comet, fuming inside. But I had underestimated the determination of the king of explosives. He ran to me, fastening a leather gun holster around his hips. Stunned, I stopped in my tracks.

"Why are you taking your weapon?"

"It's an old habit of mine because we don't know what we'll find there. We better be prepared."

"We're talking about Mack!" I said, annoyed.

He grunted and snatched the keys from my hand. I was furious.

"Where is he exactly?" he demanded.

I stared at him, placing my hands on my hips so he would understand I was not intimidated.

"Do you think I'm stupid enough to tell you so you can leave without me?"

He sighed.

"Alright. We go together. Just stay sharp—this isn't a

game."Then he shouted at Marcus from the vehicle, watching him with darting eyes."Bigma! If we're not back in an hour, call me. If I don't answer, warn Jerry."

He nodded.

"And where are we supposed to pick him up?" Ash demanded again.

"A deserted area," I replied, remaining deliberately vague.

"Get in," he ordered me after thinking for a few seconds.

I slid into the passenger seat and slammed the door just as Ash threw the car into reverse. The sudden jolt sent me gripping the door for balance. He sped toward the stop sign, then slammed the brakes. We locked eyes, both seething.

"Easy with my car! Mack isn't going anywhere!"

"Which way?" he ordered impatiently.

"This way," I said, pointing to the right.

"Thanks!"

The atmosphere became more and more electric. I could barely stand being trapped in my own car with an angry man who refused to talk.

"At the traffic lights, turn left," I said, breaking the silence after several minutes.

"Can I get the address now?"

"No. You would be able to force me out of the car and call someone to pick me up."

He sighed, trying to smile.

"What?" I asked.

"That's right. That's probably what I would do."

I groaned. I shot him a few glances and realized he was

on edge, probably even more than I initially thought. I could understand he'd be angry because of my attempt to disobey him. Was I that good at it? He was clutching the steering wheel, growing impatient at each traffic light.

"Do not forget to breathe," I whispered between my teeth.

He gave me an exasperated smile. Then, I proclaimed peace, as I could no longer bear the tense atmosphere in the car. We were about to explode–with no pun intended.

"You know, I'm not as stupid as you think..."

My eyes followed the landscape scrolling by the window, not really daring to look at his darting eyes. The shops were now scarce, and dry plains became more and more prominent. Traffic was lighter too.

"You have the right not to tell me anything. I don't know what Mack did, but I'm old enough to understand that it's serious. Even if you do not tell me anything, I hear stuff. Do you think Mack is back on drugs?"

After a few minutes, Ash looked at me, still driving like a madman.

"I never said you were stupid. Carefree, yes, but stupid, no. If we act like this, it's to protect you, Joe." He laughed. "Your father is going to kill me when he knows that I've let you come."

"Well, I'll speak to him first. I am too old to be chaperoned."

"You don't get it."

I instructed him to turn right. I felt my blood pressure rise, and my pulse quickened.

"Here we are," I whispered with less assurance than I had when we left the workshop.

Skeptically, Ash parked on the huge parking lot that I pointed out on the left.

"The old slaughterhouse?" he asked.

"Yeah..."

He typed a brief message on his phone, and I realized he was texting Marcus. That, added to the fact he had come with a gun, was enough to worry me. I could hardly breathe, but I tried to hide it from him.

"Nice place," he joked. "But he is nowhere to be seen."

"Wait," I said.

I tried to call Mack's cell, but I got his voicemail.

"Fuck!" Ash said impatiently. "This guy should get a new brain!"

"Ash..."

He calmed down and then turned to me. "You stay here."

"What?"

He opened the door and grabbed his jacket.

"Hey, where are you going? You are not going to leave me here by myself!"

"And you wanted to come alone?" he snapped at me mischievously.

He had a point.

"Don't move," he repeated. "It's an order. I want to inspect the building. At the first sign of trouble, you get the hell away from here and call Bigma."

I nodded, but my mind was blacking out. I couldn't stand the pressure. Ash closed the door, and I felt horribly lonely. I was sitting in my car, in the middle of an abandoned slaughterhouse's parking lot, all by myself, looking for an ex-junkie with an armed bad boy who was a fan of

Janice Joplin. Apart from that, everything was fine. I tried to convince myself everything would be fine.

I tried to control my breathing and watched Ash, who had already reached the main door. The building was in bad shape. The plaster was coming off, and rust was eating up the walls. With his hands on his gun, I saw him carefully duck inside. I was dead worried, and I wished I had listened to him. I wanted to play in the big league, but I was not ready yet. I was feeling like one of these little girls who put their tiny feet into their mom's stilettos, thinking they would become women instantaneously.

Ash disappeared through the door, and I could no longer see him. My heart skipped a beat. Everything would be over soon. Ash was going to find Mack, and we would all go home—safe and sound. That became my mantra for the next ten minutes. Then, the sound of a gunshot rose through the air. I almost went into cardiac arrest.

What was I supposed to do? Should I take the steering wheel and leave, as Ash had instructed me? What if the gunshot was accidental? Maybe he needed help... Mack could also be hurt. Given he was probably an addict, everything was possible... I could not leave them there! I got out of the vehicle. My legs were trembling, and my voice was shaky.

"Ash?"

I did not dare to speak louder, not knowing what was going on. I walked carefully and reached the slaughter-house door.

"Mack?"

No noise came from inside. I was extremely anxious. I

took a deep breath before walking into the darkness. I just had time to hear a scream before something pulled me back with an irresistible force.

"Joe, run!"

Ash was firmly held by a hooded guy with big muscular arms. I was not fast enough, despite my determination to get away from this place. Another thug grabbed me and restrained my hands behind my back. I saw a gun on the ground and noticed my friend's empty holster. Blood was dripping from his temple. They had hit him.

"Let her go," he screamed furiously. "She has nothing to do with this!"

His words earned him a punch in the face. I was horrified by so much violence.

"No!" I called.

I was screaming my guts out. It could not be real. A male voice rose through the darkness.

"You're wrong. We came for her."

The guy, who was wearing a perfectly cut suit, spoke with a horrible Eastern accent. He took a step forward, and I studied his face. It was chubby, and his complexion was pale. He was in his fifties. Maybe his receding hairline made him look older. I couldn't think clearly anymore. He gave me a cruel smile that made me think of a serial killer coming straight out of hell. His finger circled my face, and I was shaking with fear. Were they there for me? I did not understand. Where was Mack?

"Take her!" he ordered.

"No," I tried to say in unison with Ash.

I felt a terrible burning in my neck, and then my vision blurred.

"We got him too. Let's take him away!"

These were the last words my tired brain could figure out.

"Ash..." I tried to whisper in an ultimate prayer.

Then I blacked out.

28

JOE

I felt a reminiscent buzzing sensation in my head, and a cold draft made me shudder. I heard a distant sound growing louder and louder. My temples throbbed violently. I did not understand a word of the strange language I was hearing. I could only identify masculine voices. All I could see was darkness. Then I realized that my eyelids were closed. Reopening them proved difficult, as if something was weighing on them. A bitter taste filled my mouth. When I opened my eyes, the light blinded me as if it was directed into my face. My vision was still blurry, so I still couldn't make out where I was.

"Where...?"

The words died in my mouth. Its muscles were still sore. Had I been drugged? I couldn't think straight. I was high.

The voices grew louder, and I could accurately hear words in a language I did not understand. It sounded like an Eastern dialect.

"Ash..." I tried to articulate unsuccessfully.

I was whispering, maybe mumbling. I couldn't control my lips or my eyes, which were still blinking. It took me several minutes to visualize that I was in a dark place. The light I felt on my face came from a foot lamp located a bit further. I saw a chair facing me, and I suddenly realized I was sitting on another one. I wanted to move my hands, but they were tied behind my back. I tried to get up, but I felt dizzy. I heard a deep voice speaking to me.

"Ta, ta, ta, ta," said a voice in a reprimanding tone. "Don't move, Gorgeous."

"Where am I...?"

All I could say were these three words slowly, very slowly...

"That's not important," the man answered in a serious tone.

Then I saw him.

The man who owned the imposing voice. He was sitting right in front of me. Despite my lethargic state, I felt intimidated by his broad shoulders. He was wearing a well-tailored suit. It was undoubtedly custom-made. I recognized him. I remembered he was the man who had kidnapped me. He was the boss of the group of men who had drugged me and brought me there.

"Who are you?" I asked.

His wide jaw broke into a broad smile as he laughed. "Get her up."

Who was he talking to? I did not see his companion

since he came from behind. I felt him touch my wrists several times. Then he pulled on my ties until I could stand up. It only took a few seconds, and I had to rely on the strength of my captor's arms not to fall face down on the ground.

"Where is Ash?"

The boss shook his head with an impassive look on his face.

"You do not ask the right questions, little girl."

Another man who considered me a kid. It was annoying. I was going on thirty years old. But right then, it didn't matter.

"Bring her on the table, put her on her stomach."

"What?"

My brain was fighting against the fog that inhabited it, and when my ideas became clearer, I panicked. What table were they talking about? My heart racing, I turned my head around to scan the room. We were in an abandoned place, but it was not a slaughterhouse. Offices, maybe. There were a few scattered metal tables and chairs. Old state maps were plastered on the wall. Until that day, that place hadn't been used for a long time. I only had a few moments to try to figure out where I was.

The man pushed me violently on one of the tables until I laid flat against it. I still had no idea, or a vague one, about what was going to happen to me, and I shuddered. I noticed another guy, who was leaner and younger, in the corner of the room. He kept in hands crossed in front of him, like a good kid. Bullshit!

Brutally, Goliath pushed me harder. He clicked his tongue and spoke to the lean guy, who answered instantly.

With my cheek pressed against the table, I made an attempt to stop them from harming me.

"I do not even know you! You're making a mistake!"

They laughed.

"Oh, no, there is no mistake, Gorgeous."

His accent terrified me more than anything. A door slammed on my left, and my heart skipped a beat. Everything seemed surreal, but it got worse when I spotted Mack, restrained by the skinny guy. What was he doing there exactly? He had called me so I would come and get him. Had he fallen into the same trap? And how could such a frail guy overpower the strong, tattooed blond man? None of this was making sense, and I felt like my life was at stake.

"Mack," I groaned with my bust pressed against the table.

He raised his ice-blue eyes towards me. They shone too brightly. The skin around his eyes was red, and purple circles covered the tops of his cheeks. The braid, tied on the top of his head, was a mess.

"Mack!" I repeated louder.

He had lost his arrogance. The Eastern guy held him by the neck while he dragged his feet.

"Get away. I'll do it," grumbled the boss, just behind me.

I was finally free, but it only lasted for a few seconds, after which I felt the big boss' body pressed against my buttocks. He placed his hands on my hips to let me know I was under his control. I swallowed hard.

"Mack, who are these guys?" I yelled.

The lean man forced him to walk to my table. When

he reached it, his legs gave away, and tears flooded his face. I was stunned. It was like watching a Viking beg for mercy. It did not make any sense. It wasn't like him. I knew that under normal circumstances, he would have fought to save me! I was one of them, for god's sake! I was his friend... or so I thought. Suddenly, I wasn't sure of anything anymore. Was I there because of him? I felt completely helpless, facing a giant in tears.

"I'm sorry," he articulated, sniffling.

His face was expressing intense emotional and physical pain. I did not understand what was going on. I thought I was going crazy. Maybe I was. My inner voice was telling me to run away, but I could not.

"What do you want me to do with him, Boss?" asked the guy, who was holding Mack firmly by the collar of his t-shirt.

"You sit him here, and you tie him up. I want him to be in the front row."

I watched the handsome blond guy, whom I no longer recognized. He was hardly a man anymore. He looked like a ghost. Where was the tough biker I had known, ready to take on the world? He had become a wreck who was only able to cry and apologize for his mistakes. I had no clue what was going on, but one thing was crystal clear. They were about to harm me!

"I don't know you!" I shouted, struggling.

It didn't work. This guy's grip was too strong.

"We know your father!" he finally answered.

Shocked, I froze. All of them seemed to be acquainted with my father. Was he the missing link in all this shit?

"I have nothing to do with his business," I said

between my teeth as he pressed his hand firmly on my head.

"I couldn't care less, Gorgeous!"

Then, I heard it. It was the bloodcurdling metallic sound of a belt buckle that was being undone. When I realized what he was doing, I felt nauseous. All I could hear was my panting. The next thing I heard was the sound of a zipper. Tears came to my eyes as I realized what was going to happen. I wanted to scream and gather enough strength to fight the man, but I was helpless and devastated.

"Let go of her," Mack pleaded, sobbing.

What a coward! Was it the best he could do? I could no longer stand his beaten dog's eyes, watching helplessly what was going to happen to me.

"You promised me..." he protested.

It was then I discovered the real meaning of the word "hate." I hated him with all my strength, my body, and my heart. I glared at him. He was responsible for my fate. I was sure of it. The intense sadness I could see on his tear-flooded face was undeniable proof of his guilt!

"Fine. Are you recording?"

I was so focused on my anger that I didn't pay attention to the man walking with a phone, pointing it at us. It was the supreme humiliation. I spat at him, but as I was lying on the table, I missed my target. The bastard laughed and nodded to the boss.

"Alright. Zoom on me. I have a message to send," the boss said.

I couldn't feel my heart beating anymore. It just kept

me alive, anarchically hammering in my chest, compressed by the weight of this guy.

"Hi, Jerry," he began. "As you can see, I've found a pretty thing."

Grabbing my hair, he pulled my head back, which brought tears of pain to my eyes. I clenched my teeth, so I wouldn't throw up. This guy disgusted me.

"You took care of my brother. Now it is my turn."

His hand circled around my hips, reaching between the edge of the table and my jeans. His strong grip prevented me from moving. There was no escape. I had no choice but to star in this lousy show. He undid my jeans and slid them down my legs before pressing himself harder against me so I wouldn't try to do anything stupid. What would have been the point? There was no hope.

"I'm not going to kill her, at least not yet. Don't worry. My men and I are going to have a little fun before. If you want to see your kid alive again, you don't have a choice, Jerry. You come here, and we settle things like real men do. But I have something to show you first...."

A rough hand was sliding down the last piece of fabric covering my butt.

"And come alone. I know you understand. An eye for an eye. This is your only option if you want to get your kid back or what will be left of her when we're done."

I was devastated. A part of me was going to die on this table. This little piece of your soul withholds your pride, self-esteem, and faith in humanity.

"We also have two of your men. I am not sure what we are going to do with them yet. One of them is a crybaby. Can you see him, Jerry?"

I heard him laugh, and I felt nauseous.

"Well," he said, in a satisfied tone, "the other one is in pretty bad shape. It goes without saying that if you try anything stupid, we'll get rid of them both. Come to the intersection of Hills Road and Hampfrey at 11.00 p.m. I hope I've made myself clear."

I heard his breathing behind me and felt his raspy fingers brushing against my hips. I moaned in horror. I tried to concentrate on what I had heard. Ash was alive somewhere. It gave me a little bit of hope.

"And just in case you think I'm not serious, watch what I'm capable of."

Then, he took away the little innocence I had left. He violated my body with a perverse and barbaric pleasure. My eyes were locked on Mack's. He looked pathetic, ashamed, and overwhelmed by what he had done and the act of the man who was brutally dominating me. I kept looking at him. He became my point of focus in the darkness that surrounded me. I wanted him to watch me so he would witness the consequences of his actions and the loss of my dignity.

My body was shaking under the assaults and grunts of the man who was torturing me. Each jolt slowly dragged me away from reality. Finally, my mind gave me a break from the horror I was experiencing. It escaped far, very far away, so I could no longer feel the pain inflicted on me. I couldn't even feel his grip on my hips anymore. His grunts became whispers, and Mack's image faded in front of my eyes. My mind had left my body. I couldn't take it anymore, so I sought refuge in an imaginary and protective bubble where nothing could reach me. Then I saw her.

Her long blond locks and her angelic smile. She held out her hand to me, and I touched her fingers to beg her to take me away with her.

"Mom..."

She remained silent, but she stroked my cheek with her warm, soothing hand.

29

JERRY

Tidying up the office couldn't be delayed any longer. This place was a mess. If the guys from the IRS decided to drop by, we would be in deep trouble. I filed all the bills, at least those I could put my hand on. Mona also helped me with the accounting, but she lacked rigor, so it soon became unmanageable. I heard someone call me from the entrance door. Grunting, I lifted my stiff body out of the chair and exited my office to meet a potential client. Business was good. Our expertise in the area of vintage vehicles brought a regular flow of customers. But it was only David, the postman, a regular guy who delivered our mail every day. I greeted him politely, and he handed me a bunch of envelopes. I thanked him and wished him a good day. Despite appearances, bikers had manners.

With my small package under my arm, I went back to

my office and threw it on my desk. I noticed one of the envelopes was thicker than the others. Curious, I grabbed it first. Our parts orders were always delivered by carriers. Maybe Foxy had used the workshop address to have something sent to him. What an idiot! One time, he had a big shipment of French wine delivered to the office. We had drunk one wine case to teach him a lesson! I still laughed when I thought about it.

I opened the envelope and realized no delivery address was mentioned in the designated field. How did David know it was for us? Now, it was too late to catch up with him and ask. I would ask him tomorrow. I felt something was off, and I didn't like it. I put my hand inside and found a high-end phone. It was unexpected. Was Foxy involved in the trafficking of cell phones? I was about to put it on the desk so I could give it to give when he'd off for lunch, but I inadvertently pressed one of the keys and realized it hadn't been turned off.

If life had taught me anything, it was you should always listen to your inner voice, especially when it tells you something isn't right. I grabbed the phone and saw the small envelope on the screen, indicating there was a new message. What was going on?

Did one of my guys forget it somewhere, and a good Samaritan had sent it back to us?

I still had to figure out who was the rightful owner because it could be any one of us. I decided to open the message so I could return the phone. It would be a valid excuse to listen to a conversation that did not concern me. After all, I was the boss, and I wanted to clear up the matter quickly. This thing had just landed in my hands, and I wanted to get rid of it.

The audio message said a video had been uploaded on the device. When I opened it, the caption contained only two words: "For Jerry." I was stunned. Something was wrong, very wrong.

I took a quick breath and played the video, wishing to get it over with. At that moment, I discovered the true meaning of hell. Its whole extent. I had to face its darkest and most bestial side. The devil spoke with a fucking Russian accent, and his victim was my daughter. I hadn't cried for years, yet, at that moment, I felt like a little boy pretending to be a man. I didn't even see Billy enter the office. I fell back on my chair. Agonizing pain gripped my heart, a wound so deep that a lifetime wouldn't be enough to heal it.

I knew this corridor only too well. I recognized its aseptic smell, its old paint, and its shiny linoleum. I walked slowly with empty eyes, brokenhearted and feeling my soul had been crushed. I knocked three times on the wooden door. The metal plate fixed on it still looked new. I did not wait for an answer to enter. I had more important things to do than to follow the rules of etiquette. The woman standing behind her desk was only a few years older than Joe. She was wearing her usual strict ponytail and her brown and beige uniform. As soon as she saw me, she was startled. Apparently, few outlaws entered her office of their own free will.

"Jerry Welsh?" she said, her eyes sparkling, before walking around her desk to face me with her arms crossed on her chest.

"Sheriff Thompson, I need your help."

She was speechless, and I was starting to regret my decision to come to her. But this woman was my last chance.

"We have to join forces."

She looked at me for long seconds with her mouth open. Then she pulled herself together. The sheriff slammed the door shut behind me. We had a long conversation ahead of us, so many things to tell each other.

That day, I sat on the chair of an enemy so I could annihilate another one who was stronger and smarter. It never crossed my mind that one day, I'd be joining forces with a representative of an institution I had been running from for so long. I had no other choice.

I had to do.

For her.

* * *

WILD CROWS BIKERS SERIES
WILD CROWS
2. Revelation
MONTY VALLEY 1975
BLANDINE
P. MARTIN

You liked the ride?

You want to know what's going to happen next?

Let's read the 2nd book of the Wild Crows right now !

AVAILABLE ON AMAZON

About the Author

Blandine P. Martin is a novelist in love with life and she spreads it in her writings.

Slow burn romance takes on all its meaning in her stories where feelings are at the heart of the story, where the most beautiful love stories take the time to take hold so that each spark can be savored. A slow and delicious magic capable of overcoming all the challenges that fate will raise in the way of its characters.

Blandine likes to surprise her readers, take them away from everyday life, make them travel off the beaten track. His romances revisit the codes of the genre by bringing them freshness, modernity and intensity.

Emotions as a motor, she brings to life strong, complex,

deep characters, in search of themselves and more. Heroes and heroines who look like us.

Each of her novels is an ode to love, hope, gender equality and tolerance.

blandinepmartin.com

Acknowledgments

Marc Twain said, « they didn't know it was impossible, so they did it ».

It has been my motto, since the day I sent my first manuscript to a publisher.

I've become a well-known author in France, and decided it was time for the"Wild Crows" to cross borders. Since the saga has been successful beyond my wildest dreams, I wanted to share its story abroad, starting with the USA, which is the Wild Crows' birthplace.

This path I've taken is a bit crazy, full of dreams, and it's the next step in my writing career. To me, it is a brand-new adventure, which is exciting and somewhat frightening, at the same time.

I owe it, in part, to my translator, Kay, but also to my French followers, who have believed in this heartwarming story, since its beginning, in France: my proofreaders, my readers, and the persons close to me.

I also need to thank my fellow writers, who have been by my side, for letting me share with them my experience, my hopes, and my frequent moments of doubts! We are all a bit crazy, lost in our imaginary worlds, but I consider it to be a good thing. Imagination brightens our daily lives, and encourages us to beyond our limits. We have all crossed paths with that person, who is skeptical about our choice to write, and does not take us seriously because we've chosen to follow a different road. But there is nothing more fabulous than inventing new worlds, filled with stories and life paths.

My deepest wish is to make you feel emotions, as you follow my characters' stories. I want you to be transported to a different world, in which you can experience a wide range of feelings, far from your daily routine.

Thanks to my husband, who has been by my side for eight years, for his understanding and his support. He is an incredible man, who has put up with the long hours I spend writing. As I've been bitten by the writing bug, after we had met, he had no other choice!

Thanks to those, who inspire me, keep my passion alive, and feed my overactive imagination, that is always looking for new ideas. Thanks to all that make the road, I've chosen to follow, more pleasant. Your trustiness is priceless!

Finally, thank you for giving a chance to a French writer, who wishes nothing more than sharing Joe's adventures with you, and so much more.

Also by Blandine P. Martin

<u>Books actually ranslated in english :</u>

Wild Crows (romantic suspense saga - bikers)

Something blue (romantic comedy)

Harper Jones (bitlit)

Lord, King of the romanian streets (animal protection
documentary)